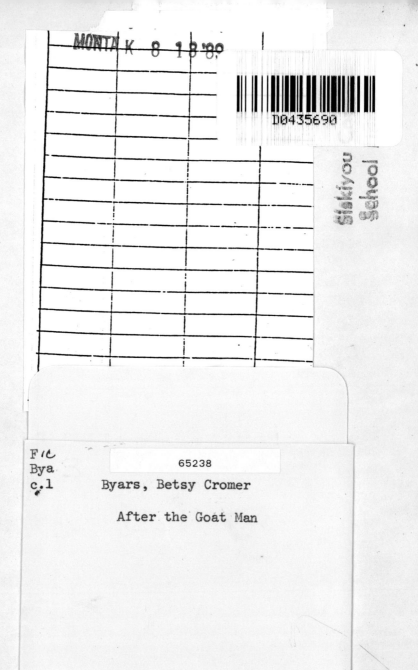

AFTER
THE
GOAT
MAN

ALSO BY BETSY BYARS

The Winged Colt of Casa Mia
The 18th Emergency
The House of Wings
Go and Hush the Baby
The Summer of the Swans
Trouble River
The Midnight Fox
Rama the Gypsy Cat

AFTER THE GOAT MAN

BETSY BYARS

Illustrated by RONALD HIMLER

THE VIKING PRESS   NEW YORK

Copyright © 1974 by Betsy Byars.
Illustrations © 1974 by The Viking Press, Inc.
All rights reserved. First published in 1974 by
The Viking Press, Inc., 625 Madison Avenue,
New York, N.Y. 10022. Published simultaneously in
Canada by The Macmillan Company of Canada Limited.
PRINTED IN U.S.A. 1 2 3 4 5 78 77 76 75 74
FIRST EDITION

LIBRARY OF CONGRESS CATALOGING IN PUBLICATION DATA

Byars, Betsy Cromer. After the goat man.
SUMMARY: An overweight sensitive boy gains
the insight and strength to overcome his problems
through his search for and discovery of a friend's
grandfather, known as the Goat Man. I. Title.
PZ7.B9836AF [Fic] 74–8200 ISBN 0–670–10908–8

CONTENTS

TEN THOUSAND
DOLLARS

The game of Monopoly had been going on for a day and a half. Two of the players were lying on their stomachs, listlessly advancing their pieces when it was their turn, resting when it was not. The third player, Figgy, was sitting up. He was bending forward, and the rabbit's foot he wore around his neck swung out over the board every time he moved. He was watching the board carefully because he owed the other two players ten thousand dollars.

The girl, Ada, slowly moved her shoe forward three places and Figgy watched. Then he jerked his head around. "Baltic Avenue, that's mine! Wait a minute, now, *wait a minute.*" There was a rule that if you didn't collect your rent promptly, you didn't get it. "Baltic Avenue, Baltic Avenue." He kept talking so no one could put the rule into effect. "Baltic Avenue. Yes, you owe me . . ." His dirty finger found the place on the card. "That will be—Do I have any houses on Baltic Avenue?"

"No."

"Then the rent will be four dollars, please."

He held out his hand, collected the money, and set it carefully in the dollar pile. Then he drank his red Kool-Aid. He liked to drink out of odd containers. It gave him an elegant feeling, and he had arranged to have Ada put his Kool-Aid in a large crystal sugar bowl. When he drank he politely held both handles. He set the sugar bowl down in front of him and said, "Whose turn is it?"

"Yours, Figgy."

"Mine?"

He did not want to take his turn because most of the board was owned by the other two players. He did not see any place he could land without going deeper into debt. He was especially fearful of landing on Boardwalk because the rent on that was two thousand dollars. He took another sip from the sugar bowl. His eyes darted around the board. He counted beneath his breath. The best thing that could happen to him, he realized, was to be sent to jail and thereby miss three turns. He took the rabbit's foot and scratched a mosquito bite on his arm with it.

Ada said, "You could get blood poisoning that way."

"How?"

"Scratching a mosquito bite with a rabbit's foot."

"No, I couldn't," Figgy said. "This is my lucky rabbit's foot."

There was a long silence while Figgy examined the board. Finally Harold said, "Go on, Figgy, take your turn."

"What's the big hurry?"

"Just go *on*."

"Well, where are the dice?"

"In front of you," Harold said wearily.

"Oh, yeah." Figgy picked up the dice and started shaking them in his cupped hands. He went on and on but nobody said anything, just let him shake the dice as much as he wanted. Harold closed his eyes and rested.

After a minute Harold got tired of hearing the dice and said, "Roll them, Figgy," in a disgusted voice. Harold shifted his weight, trying to get comfortable. There was a lot of Harold to shift this summer. He had always thought of himself as a little chubby, but now he was just plain fat and he knew it. He also knew that he wasn't going to get tall enough to thin out the fat. His mother kept saying to him, "Harold, get out of the house. Get some exercise. *Do* something. You're going to be like those twins in North Carolina."

His mother had, as a girl, known twin boys in North Carolina who grew up to weigh six hundred pounds apiece and who went into show business. She kept bringing this up, and so Harold came over to Ada's a lot to lie on her porch and play Monopoly.

He watched Figgy shaking the dice. Figgy's face was lifted. His eyes were shut. Harold said meanly, "That won't help. You're going to land on Boardwalk no matter how much you shake the dice." He paused a moment. "And that will cost you two thousand dollars."

Figgy would not jinx himself by opening his eyes. He shook the dice some more. "Don't let me land on Boardwalk," he muttered. "Let a miracle happen. Let me go to jail." He stopped shaking the dice, opened his hands slightly, and let the dice fall, one at a time, onto the board.

"Twelve," Harold cried. He counted out the move. ". . . ten, eleven, *twelve*. I told you! Boardwalk! You owe Ada two thousand dollars."

—"Two thousand . . . two thousand," Figgy repeated slowly. He looked down at his entire bankroll. Seventeen dollars.

Ada said, "You can pay me later."

"No," Harold said. "Make him pay you now. This has gone on long enough. He's in debt ten thousand dollars as it is." Harold was getting hungry. He was

miserable and he wanted to make everyone else miserable too. He said, "Oh, let's quit," and rolled over onto his back. He felt like a beached turtle.

"No, don't quit," Figgy said quickly. "I'll mortgage." He looked over his holdings rapidly. "Just don't quit, whatever you do."

"You don't have anything worth mortgaging," Harold said.

"I'll find something. Just don't quit." With one hand on his rabbit's foot, he began to shuffle through his cards.

Figgy lived a mile away-on the other side of the Boulevard in one of the houses that had been built for the people displaced by the new interstate highway, I-79. On the morning before this one, Figgy had crossed the Boulevard, come through the field, the grove of trees, walked through three yards, and had by chance come upon Ada and Harold setting up a game of Monopoly on Ada's porch. He had not even known such a game existed. "Can I play?"

Ada and Harold had not noticed him until he spoke. Then they glanced up and saw him standing at the edge of the porch watching them with his bright black eyes. He had been wearing a pair of faded brown shorts, a rabbit's foot on a string around his neck, and nothing else.

Harold had stopped setting up the bank. He said,

"Do you know how? I hate to play with people who aren't up on the rules."

"I know all the rules," Figgy had lied.

"Are you sure? You don't look like the Monopoly type."

"I know, I tell you."

Ada had said, "Oh, let him play."

Figgy had scrambled up the steps and had sat down between Harold and Ada, his back to the street. He had taken the money Harold counted out to him and arranged it in neat piles in front of him. If this was all there was, he had thought, just getting piles of money and arranging them, the game would be a success.

Now, after a day and a half, he wanted to keep playing Monopoly on Ada's porch for the rest of his life. He said, "Please, please, don't quit. Listen, I'll find something to mortgage. I *like* to mortgage."

Ada said, "Oh, you can just owe me the money. It doesn't matter."

Figgy hesitated. "Is that all right with everybody?" He looked at Harold. He knew that Harold was the one to fear. One strong word from Harold, and the game was over.

"You two keep playing if you want," Harold said, looking up at the ceiling. "I've had it." He turned over and got slowly to his feet.

"Listen, don't quit," Figgy pleaded.

Harold pulled his sweat shirt down over his stomach. He looked at Figgy. He said, "I got to go home and get ready for supper."

"It's only—" Figgy grabbed Ada's arm and looked at her watch. "It's only three o'clock."

Harold thought it could not possibly be only three o'clock. He was starving. He had been imagining that at this moment his mother was putting bowls of food on the table. He thought he had actually smelled fried potatoes. He said, "We eat early."

Figgy blinked. He said suddenly, "Then can I have your money and stuff?"

Harold said, "Divide it." Figgy dived across the board and began to gather up the money.

"Don't bother," Ada said. "I'm tired of playing too." She sat up, looked at her elbows, and brushed them off. "I'll see you later, Harold."

"Right."

Figgy sighed. He had known that Harold was the key to the game. He sat, shoulders slumped. He looked from Ada's face to Harold's back. Then he leaned forward, squinted, and said, "What's that on the front of his T-shirt?"

"It says WCLG. That's a radio station."

"Oh."

"Harold won that T-shirt."

"Really? In a contest?"

"Yes."

Walking across the lawn, Harold heard them and felt comforted by the mention of his T-shirt. He was proud of this shirt. The radio station had had a Golden Oldie contest in June, and when they played a Golden Oldie the first person to call and identify the record won a yellow T-shirt with GOLDEN OLDIE on the back and WCLG on the front. Harold had correctly identified Rick Nelson singing "Garden Party."

Figgy turned back to the game. He said, "I'll put everything away." He began separating the money carefully into piles.

"Just stuff it back in."

"No, I like to do it this way." He worked for a while, and then he said, "Are you guys going to play again after supper?"

"I don't know. It depends on Harold."

"Oh." Figgy hesitated. He took the rabbit's foot and scratched the mosquito bite on his arm. Then he said, "Well, I'll come over as soon as I eat. Then if we want to play Monopoly, we'll play Monopoly, and if we don't, we can play something else. Maybe just watch television."

Ada nodded.

"I'll see you right after supper." He finished putting the game away and ran off quickly through the yard. His skinny arms were flying out from his body. Halfway across the lawn he spun around and said, "Don't worry. I'll be right back." Then he turned and disappeared from sight.

MISSING

Figgy ran home fast. He cut through three yards, dodging the shaped bushes and trees and ducking under fences. Everything had a clean, washed look. Figgy loved yards like these, green and trimmed with white concrete walks and flowers. He thought people were lucky to have yards like these, not knowing how hard they had to work to get them.

A dog barked at him, and he took his rabbit's foot quickly in his hand and said, "It's all right. It's just me—Figgy." Because of the rabbit's foot, he didn't have any fear. "This rabbit's foot really works," he told everybody. "You should get one." But nobody seemed impressed.

He waited, rabbit's foot in hand, and after a moment the dog went back and lay down by the steps. Figgy glanced around to see if anyone had witnessed the magic. He was alone.

Walking quickly, he entered a grove of trees and then crossed the Boulevard. The pavement was hot, and he ran, pausing on the grass to ease his feet. As he paused he looked up and saw the street where he and his grandfather lived.

There were twelve houses, and he and his grandfather lived in the last one. It was exactly like the other concrete block houses except that there was no sign of life at Figgy's house. The other houses had clothes on the lines and tricycles in the yards and chairs on the porches. At his house the shades were drawn and the doors and windows were shut. To look at his house you would think it was still vacant.

Figgy began to walk the rest of the way slowly. He knew that his grandfather would be in the house sitting in the darkened front room. He would be slumped forward on the old maroon sofa, his back humped over like a bull's. He would not look up as Figgy came in.

Figgy would say, "Hi." His grandfather would not look up. Figgy could make all the noise he wanted to and his grandfather would just sit there. But if there was a noise outside, Figgy thought, if a child ran into the yard or a car turned into the graveled driveway, his grandfather would rise up. He would uncoil like a snake. He would throw open the door in one motion and cry, "Get off! Get out of here!" He would shake his fist like the weapon it was. "Get out of here! Get off!"

They had been living in this house only three days and already no children would come into the yard. The terrible, "Get off! Get out of here!" and the blackness of his grandfather's expression had sent them flying. No child ever underestimated his grandfather. No child ever thought, "Oh, well, he's just bluffing. Let's go on in his yard anyway." No child ever said, "Let's go in his yard, want to? And watch him yell at us?" The children would ride their tricycles up to the edge of the yard and then turn quickly and speed down the hill, their legs spinning faster than the wheels.

"Get off! Get out of here!" That was all Figgy could remember hearing from his grandfather for the past two years. It started the day they had first learned about the new highway.

It had been September, and a man had come up to their cabin, which was on the side of a hill below the old coal mine. The man had told them about the new superhighway that was going to come through the valley. Right where the cabin was sitting, he told them, was going to be a giant cloverleaf turnoff.

Figgy had been struck with excitement. He had hopped up and down, saying, "Did you hear that? There's going to be a superhighway!" He felt as if a new holiday had been invented. "A superhighway!"

His grandfather was so silent Figgy thought he had not understood the man. "Grandpa, there's going to be a giant cloverleaf turnoff right here on this very spot." He had glanced up, had seen his grandfather's face, and his words had trailed into silence.

His grandfather had grown. He had actually gotten bigger in size. He had swelled up like a frog while Figgy was hopping with excitement. He was bigger than life now, something carved out of the mountain, big and hard as granite, except for his arms, which were trembling a little.

Figgy said, "Grandpa," in a worried way. "Grandpa, listen." He stopped and squinted up at the strange highway man, waiting.

There was a silence. Then his grandfather's voice came out as deep as if it were coming from a cave. "Get out. Get *out!*"

The man fell back a few steps. He stopped and said, "Sir, I am only trying to help you by—"

"Get off! Get out of here! This is my land!" It was like thunder rumbling down the sides of the mountain. "This is *my land!*"

That had been to Figgy an all-powerful, indisputable statement. He had seen enough of forest life to know about an animal's territory, and how animals fought to the death to protect it. He saw now it was the same with his grandfather.

"Sir, you—"

"No highway's going on *my land.*"

"Sir—"

"Never!"

There was another silence, and Figgy said to the man, "He means it." He said it because he wanted to spare the man the trouble of coming back. Nobody would get his grandfather's land. He felt a little sorry for the man as he walked away to his truck.

It had taken the highway department two years, but they had done it. And in those two years his grandfather had changed. He had started going around muttering to himself about the land. Figgy would come up the path and bump right into his grandfather, and his grandfather wouldn't see him, just pass by muttering about highways and deeds and a man's rights.

Or in the middle of supper his grandfather would rise and go outside and disappear into the trees. Or in the dark of night his grandfather would wake up, yelling, sending imaginary men and trucks and bulldozers away with just the strength of his voice.

In the end his voice had not been enough, and

Figgy and his grandfather had to leave their cabin. When the truck came for them, his grandfather had stood by, looking down at the ground, silent and worn-down, while their furniture was loaded on the truck.

Figgy had been surprised by this sudden and awful stillness. He had expected his grandfather to explode when the men lifted the first stick of furniture. Instead he had just stood there, and when they told him to get in the truck, he did, and he sat without moving while the truck drove away through the cleared land.

Sitting by his grandfather, holding the old Philco radio on his lap, Figgy had thought that perhaps everything was going to be all right. Maybe his grandfather secretly wanted to live in the new house just as he did. Maybe this was the beginning of a new life for both of them in that modern world of water from silver spigots and heat from pipes in the wall.

For two days Figgy had hoped. He had stayed in the house with his grandfather, trying to interest him in the new appliances. On the third day, however, he had given up, gone out, and found the game of Monopoly.

Figgy walked up the street. He felt good. He wished his grandfather could find something like Monopoly. He had suggested that his grandfather sit out on the porch and watch the traffic go by on the Boulevard. There was an old lady down the street who spent most of the day in a straight chair on the porch admiring traffic, but his grandfather wouldn't even try it.

Figgy passed a house where three little children were in a blue plastic swimming pool. They were screaming because a two-year-old named Willie was scooping out water in his hands and throwing it on the ground.

"Mama, look what Willie's doing!"

"Mama, he's taking all our water!"

Encouraged, Willie tried to lift one side of the plastic pool and topple them out.

"Mama, he's going to turn us over!"

"Mama, look what Willie's doing!"

Figgy walked to his house. He would have liked living in this house, he would have liked the whole neighborhood if it weren't for his grandfather. It was the nicest house Figgy had ever lived in. He couldn't see why his grandfather hated it.

He came up on the porch and turned the door-knob. The door was locked. There was a square of glass in the door and he looked in.

"Grandpa, you in there?"

There was no answer.

Figgy walked slowly around the house, stopping to peer in each window. There was a little slit beneath the shades, but he couldn't see anything. He tried the back door. It was locked too.

He rattled the doorknob. "Grandpa!" He pressed his face to the glass, shielding it with his hands. "Grandpa!"

From the back door, he could see the kitchen and on into the living room, but his grandfather was not in sight. Just to the left of the front door was the sofa, and his grandfather always sat there on the sagging center cushion. The sofa was empty.

"Grandpa!" He rattled the doorknob and beat his fist on the door. "Hey, Grandpa, it's just me." He put his hand on the rabbit's foot.

"Honey." He looked around, startled, and saw the woman from next door. She was standing by her clothesline, wiping her hands on her apron. "Your grandfather's not home. He went off."

"What?"

"Your grandfather went off," she said. "It was about an hour ago. I just happened to look out the window and see him walking down the street."

"Where was he going? Did he say?"

"He never said a word to anybody. He just came out of the house and walked right down the street without so much as looking right or left. You could have struck a match on his face."

Figgy knew that look. He said, "Oh."

"I thought he might have been going hunting because he had his gun with him, but Bert says it's not hunting season."

The good feeling kept leaving Figgy. "His shotgun," he said. It was not a question, but the woman nodded. Figgy kept standing there because he didn't know what else to do.

There was a little boy behind the woman, and he leaned around her skirt and said to Figgy, "Your grandfather is the Goat Man."

"Hush up," the woman said.

"Well, he is, Mom."

"Hush!" She looked at Figgy and said, "If you want to get in your house, honey, you can use my key because all the locks are the same. They're going to change them, but they haven't got around to it yet."

She got the key for him, and Figgy opened the door without speaking. Behind him the little boy said again, "Well, his grandfather is *too* the Goat Man. Ask Daddy if you don't believe me."

"I thought I told you to hush."

"Here," Figgy said. He handed her the key and went into the house. It was dark and hot and stuffy, and he walked slowly from one empty room to another. His grandfather was gone, all right.

Figgy went slowly back into the kitchen. He had planned on eating something as quickly as possible

and getting back over to Ada's for the Monopoly game. Now he wasn't hungry.

He opened the refrigerator and looked inside. There wasn't much to eat anyway. He took out a bottle of ice water and poured some into a glass. Then he remembered the wonderful crystal sugar bowl he had been permitted to drink out of at Ada's, and he started looking for a more imaginative container.

Finally he came across the small blue pitcher with a crack in it. He filled it with ice water, dropped a Fizzy in and waited. When the Fizzy dissolved, he turned up the pitcher and slowly drank out of the spout. With his free hand he held on to his rabbit's foot.

OVER AND OUT

Harold was making a list of things he wanted never to see or hear on television again. He said, "You know, it's strange. You think there are millions of things you don't want to see on television until you start trying to make a list."

"I hardly ever watch television any more."

"Well, me either," Harold lied. He had a television set in his room, and he sometimes went to sleep watching the late movie and woke up to Sunrise Semester.

Harold bent over his list and began to write. He and Ada had been sitting on the porch for thirty minutes listening to Ada's transistor radio. Harold was marking time until Figgy came, by making the list.

Ada put her long black hair behind her ears and leaned forward to look at Harold's list. "What have you got so far?"

"Nothing much. I'm just writing some general things I hate on television, like people not really singing songs but just moving their lips to a record—things like that—and canned laughter. Faked stuff. When I get enough I'm going to write the networks."

"Put down toy commercials," Ada said, "if you're putting down fake stuff."

"Right." Instantly Harold began to write it down. He was sorry he hadn't thought of it himself. "I used to be taken in by those all the time. I saw a truck on TV one time—Big Mack—and it was going over mountains and through dirt walls and crushing boulders and I couldn't wait to get it. I was going to destruct the whole neighborhood."

"Fake?"

"On Christmas morning I couldn't get it to start without a push and it couldn't even crawl over the seam in the carpet. It was my biggest Christmas disappointment." He glanced back at his list. "Either that or my walkie-talkies."

"What happened with them?"

"Well, the year I got them I didn't know anybody, and so my family had to be on one walkie-talkie in the living room while I went all over the neighborhood with the other. They would say, 'Where are you

now, Harold?' and I'd say, 'I am at the Waltons'
driveway.' And they would say, 'We hear you loud
and clear.' I'd say, 'Roger. Over and out.' I had all
the phrases, see, I was cool on those walkie-talkies.
Then I'd go about four steps and say, 'I am at the
Todds' driveway now. How do you hear?' And
they'd say, 'Loud and clear.' I'd say, 'Roger. Over and
out.' Then I had to know how they heard me at the
Morgans' driveway. 'Roger. Over and out.' And at
the Hunters'. I suppose I would have kept on and on
except that old man Hunter came out and hollered
at me and asked when I was going to get through with
the walkie-talkies. He said I was interfering with his
televison. My voice was *broadcasting!* All my 'Rogers'
and 'over and outs' were being *broadcast.* By some
fluke of the air waves my voice was being transmitted
into every home in the neighborhood. I never en-
joyed my walkie-talkies after that."

Ada grinned and put her hair behind her ears
again. "I've had some Christmas disappointments myself." Then she straightened and said, "Listen, I
wonder what's keeping Figgy."

"I don't know. I'm beginning to hope he doesn't
come. We've been playing Monopoly for two days
now. There's such a thing as too much Monopoly."

"I like to play."

"Well, I do too for an hour or so." He sighed suddenly and put the list down. "I'm tired of doing this," he said.

"What's wrong?"

"Nothing. I'm just tired of the list, that's all." What was really wrong was that all he had had for supper was a fruit salad and he was hungry. He did not want to tell Ada because he knew she would not understand.

He remembered that he had once gone to the Dairy Queen with Ada and had stood there while she looked at the bright, beautiful pictures of ice cream concoctions. She had shifted her weight from one foot to the other. The two dollar bills in his hands were getting damp. He could never remember offering a waitress money that wasn't moist.

"What do you want, Ada?" he kept asking impatiently.

Finally she had said, "Oh, I don't know. I guess I'll have a—Oh, just get me a small vanilla cone."

He could not believe his ears. "Don't you want a Fiesta?" he had said. That was the grandest thing this Dairy Queen had to offer. They put every single thing they had on it.

"Nobody but goops get those."

"Oh." He was at the window by this time all ready to say, "One Fiesta, please," to the girl behind the window. Now he hesitated. He could have wept. He said,

"Oh, well, I'll just take a vanilla cone too." He started to turn away, but then he swirled around and added quickly, "Make mine a large cone and dip it in chocolate and decorettes," but he was still disappointed. Then to climax the whole thing Ada had taken two licks of her cone and fed the rest to a stray dog who was waiting by the carry-out window. Somebody like Ada could never understand real hunger.

He shifted his weight and looked at his watch. Ada said, "It's seven o'clock because the news is on." She paused, listened for a minute.

Harold said, "The announcer always sounds so cheerful when the news is bad. Have you ever noticed that?"

"Yes." She leaned forward on her arms.

Harold imitated the announcer. "Tonight I'll bring you news of a sea disaster, a flood, a fire, and a mass murder right after this word for people who want to shed those extra pounds." He gave Ada a quick look to see if she was going to comment on the commercial he had made up. He hadn't meant to say that. But Ada was looking down at her arms.

"In the headlines again this evening," the announcer was saying, "is the Goat Man, Ira Gryshevich, who came into prominence last year when he refused to leave his house to make way for Highway I-79. After a long and bitter struggle the Goat Man was put out of his home, but he has now surprised highway officials by moving back into the empty cabin with a gun and he has threatened to shoot anybody who tries to get him out. Highway officials have no comment at this time."

"Yay for the Goat Man," Ada said. "I hope they never get him out. I hope they have to build the high- way around him. Zoop, zooooop, zoop." In the air she drew a long straight highway with a horseshoe bump in it.

"Oh, they'll get him out one way or another," Harold said. "They'll starve him out or use tear gas or something. Mace maybe."

They sat without speaking, listening to the music that had come on after the news. Suddenly Harold sat up and said, "Well, here comes Figgy at last. Get the game out. I'll be the banker."

Figgy came around the side of the house on the run. He stood there at the foot of the steps, panting for breath, holding his rabbit's foot in one hand. He said, "I can't play. I just came over to tell you."

Harold said in an irritated voice, "We've been hold- ing up the game for you."

"Well, I can't play, that's all." He threw out his skinny arms in a gesture of helplessness. "I just can't *play*."

THE GOAT MAN

Ada waited a moment and then she said, "Is there any special reason, Figgy? Do you have to go somewhere?"

"No, I just can't play." Figgy hesitated. He squinted up at Ada. He did not know how much to tell.

The trouble with his grandfather had been a source of pain to Figgy during the past year. His grandfather had been, up until the trouble over the highway, a stern but gentle man, a sort of hermit. He had been known, not unkindly, as the Goat Man.

This name had gotten started because of the goats, two of them, that followed his grandfather everywhere. The goats were like dogs. They would follow his grandfather to the store and wait outside until he came out with the groceries. They would run after him when he called and stop when he told them to stop.

His grandfather had loved those goats. They were his friends in a way nobody else had ever been.

The two goats had died within a month of each other. Figgy had found the oldest goat in the ravine one morning. The goat had eaten something poisonous. They never found out what it was, but his eyes had been spinning around in his head like pinwheels, and by the time his grandfather got there, the goat Brownie was dead.

The second goat, Pepper, was the stupider of the two and had managed to survive through the years by following Brownie's lead. One day, three weeks later, Pepper ran out in the road in front of the grocery store and was struck by a gravel truck. He was killed instantly.

After that people still continued to call his grandfather the Goat Man and the name seemed a kind thing to Figgy. It was later that it became an insult. When the newspapers wrote about him and the radio told about him, when people pointed to him on the street and said, "Look, there's the Goat Man," it didn't seem kind at all.

Now as Figgy stood looking at Harold and Ada, he wondered if he should tell these new friends, by far the most fascinating he had ever known, about his grandfather. He was afraid Harold would cry, "You mean *your* grandfather's the *Goat Man!*"

"Well, if you don't *want* to play," Harold said. He

was a sensitive person and took everything as a personal insult.

Figgy said, "Oh, it's not that. I *want* to play. I want to play more than anything." He glanced down at the game with real longing. He hesitated, looked at Ada for support, and then said in a rush, "What's happened is that my grandfather's missing and I don't know where he is or what I'm supposed to do or anything." Then he squinted at them as if to see them a little clearer, to see whether they understood or not.

Harold and Ada said, "Oh," at the same time. Both of them looked puzzled.

Ada said, "I don't understand. Do you live with your grandfather or is he visiting you or what?"

"I live with him."

"Who else lives with you?"

"Nobody. It's just me and him."

Harold said, "How about your mother and father?"

Figgy said, "Well, my mom is dead."

Ada said, "Oh," as if she had been struck with a thorn. Then she glanced quickly at Harold and said, "Mine is too."

Figgy said, "And I don't know where my dad is, and I have an aunt named Bena in Michigan, but I don't know where. Or maybe it's Minnesota. I get those two mixed up. Anyway, it's some state that starts with an M. I *know* that." He tugged his rabbit's foot for emphasis.

Harold cleared his throat and said, "How long has your grandfather been missing?"

"Since this afternoon."

"This afternoon! Is that all?" Harold said. "He's probably at the store or gone to town. He could be tied up in traffic."

Figgy shook his head. "Not my grandfather. For three days, ever since we moved into this new house, he's been sitting there, staring. He hasn't even eaten. Then when I went home for supper this afternoon he was gone."

Harold sat up straight and said, "Well, have you thought of calling the police?"

Figgy said, "No."

"That's probably the first thing you should do then," Harold said. "I'll make the call for you."

Harold loved to make important calls. If anyone in the family had to call to complain about service or to report some difficulty, Harold would always ask to make the call for them. He could make his voice very deep and important. "This is Harold V. Coleman," he would say, "and I would like to report that a telephone line is down on our street." Lately because of these telephone successes, he had thought of becoming a radio announcer. He had even sent off in secret a coupon he had found in a magazine for people who wanted to leave their humdrum jobs for a career in radio.

When Harold was younger he had thought mostly about becoming an astronaut. Landing on the moon and walking in space had filled his dreams, along with splashdowns and red carpets and parades. Then one day he had found himself on the high diving board at Marilla Pool for the first time. He had climbed up mainly to see what the view was like from up there and he had not intended to jump off at all.

While he was standing there admiring the view, however, a line of kids had formed on the ladder behind him. The first time he noticed the line was when one kid said, "Go ahead. *Dive.*" Then it was, "What are you waiting for out there—*Christmas?*"

Playing for time, Harold had said in an even and mature voice, "I'll go as soon as there aren't any little kids under the diving board."

He saw that retreating down the narrow, crowded ladder was going to be impossible. He waited. His throat had gone dry. His blood was pumping hard in his throat. All too quickly the little kids swam out of the way.

"Go ahead!"

"Dive, will you?"

"What's wrong with him, anyway?"

He had to jump.

He did not get to see the impact, of course, but everyone who did see it said there had never been such a splash since the pool had opened in 1960. People standing ten feet away got drenched. Harold had, it turned out, spun a little in the air after he left the diving board and landed flat on his back.

While he was lying in the grass that day, recuperating, it came to him that he had better not count on becoming an astronaut any more. He went over the moon landing in his mind. He saw himself standing on the ladder, getting ready to take that giant step for mankind. He saw himself jumping off the ladder and then—this was the bad part—he saw himself spinning a little, landing flat on his back and sinking deep into the moon dust. The only thing TV viewers would be able to see would be a Harold V. Coleman-shaped hole in the moon's surface, like a weird crater.

The other astronauts would dig him out, but the Harold V. Coleman crater would remain, as much a part of the moon as the Sea of Tranquillity.

As he lay at the pool that day, trying to get his mind off his stinging back, he went over the other things he couldn't be. He had thought of being a cowboy once, mainly because of the outfits, but he now realized that the only fat cowboys he had ever seen were driving the chuck wagon. He couldn't be a baseball player because unless he got a home run, a miracle that had happened only once in his life, he would always be thrown out at first. He couldn't do anything that required speed or physical skill or firm muscles. The only thing left to him was radio announcing.

"What are you going to tell the police?" Figgy was asking. He was anxiously twisting his rabbit's foot around and around. "I don't think my grandfather would want me calling the police."

"Have you got a piece of paper, Ada?" Harold asked. "Oh, I'll use the back of my list." Then he turned to Figgy. "Now, we'll just tell the police that your grandfather's missing. Maybe he's been in an accident or something and you can stop worrying."

Harold clicked his ball point pen into writing position. "All right now, let me get all the information." This was the reason his calls were so effective, he thought. He never dialed until he had all the information before him.

He rested the paper on his knee. "What is your grandfather's name?" He waited with the ballpoint pen poised over the paper.

"Well," Figgy said, "his name is Ira Gryshevich."

"Spell that, please."

Slowly, letter by letter, Figgy spelled out the name. He looked down the street where a man was cutting his grass.

Then Figgy hesitated. He looked at Harold, at Ada. He said, "But everybody calls him the Goat Man."

A PLAN

Without raising his head Harold looked over at Ada. His cheeks had gotten very pink and Ada's eyes were as blue as marbles. For a moment those seemed to be the only spots of color on the porch. Neither Ada nor Harold spoke. The news bulletin they had just heard on the radio went, word for word, through both of their minds.

Figgy had been watching for some kind of reaction, and he noticed their expressions. He said quickly, "Maybe you read about my grandfather in the newspaper or something? Is that it?"

"Well, yeah," Harold said. "I did see his picture in the paper a while back."

One Sunday when the trouble first began, there had

been a whole page of pictures of Figgy's grandfather in the Sunday newspaper. A photographer had posed Mr. Gryshevich all over his land—in front of the cabin, by the creek where he fished, beneath the hundred-and-fifty-year-old tree behind the cabin.

The pictures were all alike, and as Harold had looked at them that Sunday morning while he was waiting for his sister to get through with the comics, he had thought the photographer could have taken a cutout figure of the Goat Man and pasted it on different backgrounds and gotten the same results. No matter where the Goat Man stood he was stiff as a board, his eyes staring down at the ground.

It had made Harold a little sad. The pictures, he knew, would not help the Goat Man keep the cabin and the land, but would instead make people cry, "Get him out of the way of I-79. We want progress!"

Harold cleared his throat. "Look, Figgy. Ah, listen." He didn't think he was going to be able to continue. He realized suddenly that he liked to give out important news on the telephone but not to people's faces.

He hesitated, glanced at Ada for help, and she said, "Go on, Harold, *tell* him," in a low voice.

"Tell me what?" Figgy swung his head around quickly, looking from one to the other.

Harold hesitated again, and Ada said, "Go *on*."

"What are you going to tell me?" Figgy asked. "Is it something about my grandfather?"

"Yes. Well, it's nothing, really," Harold said, looking down at his feet. "It was just that we heard something on the radio about your grandfather. It was right before you got here."

"What?"

"Well, your grandfather has gone back to your old house, that's all, and he's locked himself in." Harold looked at Ada because he wanted to see if she thought he had told it as badly as he did. He thought maybe he wouldn't be a news reporter after all, because it seemed to him that he had a desire to make a disaster seem unimportant. He didn't want people to worry. He imagined himself on the air. "And now," a voice would say, "with the news of the worst hurricane in the history of the United States, here is Harold V. Coleman." And then he would come on and say, "Well, it's really nothing. It's just that this hurricane, or bad storm, whichever you want to call it, has knocked down a few houses and the water has ruined some trees and things. That's all. And now back to Walter Cronkite."

Reporting like that would make people feel a lot better, he thought, but he knew that a reporter should *enjoy* standing up to his neck in the rising waters. He should *love* holding the microphone out to a drowning man and asking, "Sir, how does it feel to be one of the hundred and twenty people who are drowning in this terrible hurricane?"

Figgy was staring at Harold. He said, "What did you say?"

"Your grandfather's gone back to your cabin."

"But he couldn't go back there. Our cabin's been torn down."

"No, it's *going* to be torn down. They were all ready to do it, I imagine, when he got there," Harold said. "Anyway I guess they can't tear it down with him in there. That would be murder."

Ada shot him a look from beneath her dark lashes. She said in a low voice, "He took a gun with him, though, Figgy, you ought to know that." Then she didn't look at either one of them.

Figgy said, "I know." Then he sighed and added, "Well, that's that." Then he realized he couldn't think of anything else to say. Neither could Harold or Ada, and a dark feeling settled over the three of them.

Finally Harold shrugged and said, "These things just happen, that's all." He thought that would be the way he would end his news program. For a moment the thought of his own face on the television screen saying, "These things just happen, that's all, and a pleasant good evening to all of you," blocked out what was happening on the porch.

Figgy nodded quickly. Then he said, "Well, I guess

I better go out there and see what's going on. My grandfather might shoot somebody or something. There's no telling what he might do, really. The cabin and the land are very important to him."

"But they gave him a new house, didn't they? And new land?" Harold asked.

"Yeah, but it's not the same."

Harold said, "But it's better and newer and every-thing, isn't it?"

Figgy shrugged his skinny shoulders. "It's just not the *same*."

There was another silence and then Harold asked, "Your grandfather didn't ever shoot anybody before, did he?"

"Not that I know of," Figgy said. "Anyway, he never *had* to shoot anybody. People just don't bother my grandfather much. They sort of know, see, not to fool with him. I know he wouldn't hurt *me,* and yet I wouldn't ever do anything to make him mad. That's just the way he makes you feel. You don't *want* to make him mad."

Harold looked at Figgy, and it was as if he were seeing him for the first time. Figgy was smaller than Harold had originally thought, thin and very dirty. Figgy looked back at Harold with his wide dark eyes and absently scratched at the mosquito bite with his rabbit's foot.

Ada said suddenly, "Listen we'll go out to the cabin

with you." She put the top on the Monopoly game.
"Won't we, Harold?"

"Well, yeah, sure," Harold said. He paused. "How
are we going to get there, though? We can't walk. I
know I can't." He glanced at Figgy apologetically.
"I'm not very athletic."

"You don't have to be athletic to walk," Ada said.
"Babies walk."

"Yes, but not for miles." Harold was self-conscious
about his slowness at anything athletic. In his school
in gym class when the boys were choosing teams for
baseball or basketball, he was always the last to be
chosen, he and Homer Ferguson who had bad ankles
and was not allowed to run. He said, "We could take
a cab."

Ada said, "Nobody but goops take cabs."

"Oh, well, sure," he agreed quickly, "but in an
emergency—"

"We're going to walk. Just wait while I leave a note
for my dad."

"Well, I better let my mom know too."

Harold got to his feet as Ada went into the house,
and he started across the street. He knew all he would
have to do was open the front door and call, "Mom,
I'm going off."

"Not to the Dairy Queen, Harold," she would
answer.

"All right," and that would be it. She never asked where he was going, and he thought that was because he was too big and slow to get far, like a box turtle he had once had. Harold could put that turtle down in the yard, go into the house, make a sandwich, watch something on television, talk on the telephone, and come back, and the turtle would just be coming out of its shell.

Ada went into the kitchen and got a piece of chalk. There was a framed blackboard where she left messages for her father. There was a note from yesterday saying she had gone off with Harold. She added, "And Figgy." Then she wrote, "We're going to see about Figgy's grandfather, the Goat Man."

Her face was flushed with excitement. She ran into the front bedroom and called out the window to Harold, "Hey, I just had a great idea. Why don't we go on our bikes? We could ride on the new highway. It's not open to traffic yet, but we could ride our bikes on it."

Across the street Harold was standing waiting for his mom to answer. The cat Omar had come out of the bushes, rubbed against the back of Harold's leg, and was now on Harold's shoulder.

"Yeah, fine. I'll get my bike and be over in a minute." The suggestion about the bicycles pleased Harold. The new empty highway stretched out in his mind like the yellow brick road, and he saw the three of them riding off to find happiness. We're *off* to see the Goat Man . . .

"Mom," he called again, "did you hear me? I'll be back later."

He let Omar rest on his shoulder for a moment while he waited for her answer. Then he sighed and said, "No, I am *not* going to the Dairy Queen." He put Omar down and started for his bicycle. Then, abruptly, he changed his mind and went quietly into the house.

Ada leaned out the front door and said, "Figgy, you can take my old bicycle. It still works. Meet me down at the garage."

Then she ran through the house and down into the basement where the bicycles were kept. She rolled out her new bicycle and then the old one and stood in the shadow of the garage waiting for Figgy.

"Down here, Figgy," she called. "Come on down." She leaned on the seat of her bicycle and stretched her feet out into the warm sunlight. "Figgy, come on down."

TO MAKE
ADA LAUGH

While Ada was waiting by the garage and Harold was putting his cat in the house, Figgy was running silently down the street. He glanced over his shoulder, cut through a yard, zigzagged around a tree, and kept going.

It was the mention of the bicycle that had done it. Bicycles terrified Figgy. He had been on a bicycle only once in his life and that had been a nightmare.

A few years before, Figgy had seen a bicycle leaning against the side of the A & P. He had hesitated for a moment, and then, on an impulse, he had gotten on it. He just wanted to see how it felt to be on a bicycle, and while he was standing there, holding onto the warm handlebars, he had suddenly surprised himself by pushing off with one foot and starting to pedal.

Instantly the bicycle began to swerve in a terrible twisting way, to wind, to weave in a snakelike path around the grocery store parking lot. The bicycle seemed to have a will of its own. Figgy was helpless. He thought that he would still be twisting around the parking lot if he had not had the good fortune to run into the side of a white Volkswagen.

Unfortunately he did this at the same moment that the owner of the Volkswagen came out of the store. The woman saw the accident and hollered at him. "What did you do to my car? Wait a minute, you."

Figgy dropped the bicycle and started to run.

"Get that boy! Somebody stop him!" She turned to the carry-out boy. "Get him! He's dented my car." The boy hesitated and the woman screamed, *"Get him!"*

The carry-out boy started to run after Figgy, but he was still carrying the lady's groceries. The lettuce bounced out of one bag and some lemons out of the other, and finally the boy had to stop. "I'm sorry, lady, I couldn't get him."

No one could have caught him. Figgy ran like a streak of lighting, jagging through strange yards, not even pausing to glance over his shoulder. Finally he had thrown himself under a wisteria bush and waited until his breathing got back to normal.

He had wondered as he lay there, looking up at the heavy clusters of purple flowers, how people managed to keep bicycles under control. How did they manage to just tool around in such an easy and casual manner, often with no hands? Figgy did not know, but he made a silent vow never to get on a bicycle again.

He ran faster now, just thinking about it. "They're not getting me on any bicycle," he muttered to himself. "Nobody is."

When Figgy was five blocks from Ada's house and he could see for sure that no one was following him, he slowed down to a jog. His rabbit's foot was knocking against his chest and he took it and held it in one hand.

This rabbit's foot had come out of a gum machine once by itself. Figgy had been walking in front of the Third Street store where the gum machines were, and suddenly he heard a little noise. He looked and this rabbit's foot was lying there in the slot. He could not believe his eyes for a moment. It was the first free thing he had ever gotten in his life, and this convinced him that it really was a lucky rabbit's foot. He had never been without it since.

He slowed to a walk, still holding the rabbit's foot. Then, after a while, he began to jog again. He continued at this pace, walking and then jogging, through the neighborhood of nice houses with green lawns, past the Dairy Queen, the gas station, into a neighborhood of old homes and old grass.

He passed a house with a dirt yard—he could see the broom marks on it—and then a line of houses with dirt yards that nobody swept, and then he came to a vacant house. With a sigh of relief he went up and sat on the steps and rested. He slumped forward, and his rabbit's foot hung between his knees.

As he sat there he thought about his grandfather. It was the first time he had allowed the thought to develop, and now in his mind he saw his grandfather back in the old deserted cabin. His grandfather would be standing by the door, leaning against the wall, holding his gun at his side. All the furniture would be gone, even his grandfather's old rocker, and so his grandfather would have to stand there all night. It would not be the first night his grandfather had stood, guarding the house.

Figgy didn't like to think about those last days and nights at the cabin. The land had been cleared around the cabin. The trees were gone. The cabin was in the hot sun during the day, and the drone of trucks and bulldozers was constant. A layer of dust as thick as a wool carpet lay on the floor.

There had been nothing Figgy could do, and it gave him a miserable feeling. His grandfather was the only person in the world to whom Figgy was tied. Figgy sometimes thought of other people as being all wound together as if they were caught in one huge spider web. He had only one tie, like a rowboat, and that was to his grandfather.

He was suddenly chilly. He was wearing only his

shorts and his rabbit's foot, and he got up quickly and started jogging again. He left the city. As he jogged, he wondered what Ada and Harold were doing. They were probably playing Monopoly again or maybe riding their bicycles. He wished he could be with them, pedaling along between them as if riding a bicycle were the most natural thing in the world. The three of them riding together made a pretty enough picture in his mind to put on a postcard.

Harold, he thought, was probably making Ada laugh right now. Figgy could see Ada laughing. She had small pointed teeth, and she was usually very serious, but sometimes Harold could make her laugh. Figgy had never been able to do it, but Harold could. When she laughed, she got prettier.

Figgy remembered how she had laughed when Harold told about the time he had been in a piano recital when he was five. Harold had, he claimed, forgotten the ending of the piece and played the beginning through seventeen times before his teacher, Miss Prunty, came up on the stage and led him away.

"I can just see you," Ada had said, laughing, putting her hair back behind her ears.

"Well, it wasn't funny, it was sad," Harold had said, but Figgy could tell he was pleased she was laughing.

"I can just *see* you, that's all," Ada had said. "When you tell me something I can always *see* it."

"I had on a Buster Brown suit, if that makes the picture any clearer. My orthopedic shoes completed the outfit."

"Harold, don't tell me any more," she laughed. She was all but begging for mercy from his humor now. Figgy had just sat there, looking from one to the other.

"All right," Harold said. "I *was* going to tell you about the dance recital the next year, but if you don't want to hear about it . . ."

"Harold! Tell me about the dance recital!"

"No. You'll laugh."

"I promise I won't. What did you do—tap-dance?" The thought of Harold doing a tap dance made her double over the Monopoly board. "Harold, *did* you tap-dance?"

"Well, it wasn't just a *plain* tap dance."

Ada's eyes were very bright. She waited. She didn't even seem to be breathing.

"Well," Harold went on, "it was a *military* tap, and Buddy Brian and Poindexter Watts and I represented the three branches of the service. I was navy." Then he had to stop because Ada was laughing so hard she had to wipe her eyes on her shirt.

It hadn't seemed so funny to Figgy, but Ada had laughed about it for a long time and even begged Harold to tell it twice. "Please, Harold, tell me one more time."

"Well, there's nothing to tell," Harold had said.

"Oh, yes, except that on our final buck-and-wing we brought out little American flags. We got more applause than anybody."

Later, after some thought, Figgy had said, "You know what happened to me once?" He wanted to make Ada laugh in the same way Harold had. Ada had said that no one could make her laugh except Harold, not even comedians on television, but Figgy had decided to try.

"What?" Ada asked.

Figgy had then told a long fictitious story about something that had happened to him in a school play. He had forgotten his lines, he told Ada, and the teacher had to say them for him. But it wasn't funny. Ada hadn't laughed at all, only smiled and said, "Oh, Figgy." Maybe the trouble was that he had never been chosen to be in a school play.

At the time he wondered if he would ever get to know Ada and Harold well enough to make them laugh. He felt now that it would never happen. He would never sit on Ada's porch again and play Monopoly. He would never get to speak into Harold's tape recorder. He would never get to drink out of the crystal sugar bowl. He would never make Ada laugh.

Clutching his rabbit's foot, he began to run a little faster.

WAAAAA!

Harold came out of the house eating a stalk of celery. He had told his mother he was going off with Ada, and then, before he left, he had made a silent trip into the kitchen. As soon as he had opened the refrigerator door, however, even though he had not made a sound doing it, his mother had called from upstairs, "Harold, are you eating again?"

"Again!" he cried. "What do you mean *again?* I haven't had anything since supper."

While he had been shouting this, she had come downstairs and slipped into the kitchen so quietly he hadn't heard her. He was reaching into the freezer compartment where his sister kept an assortment of frozen candy bars.

"No candy bars, Harold," she said right by his ear.

"I'm *not* getting a candy bar," he snapped, startled.

"Well, you're—"

"I was *getting* a piece of *celery*." His hand had just closed around a frozen Mound. He could not release it for a moment. His brain actually refused to relay the command to his hand. Then with a sigh he withdrew his empty hand from the freezer. He opened the crisper and snapped off a piece of celery. He slammed the refrigerator door.

"You better wash it, Harold."

"Why? Is dirt fattening too?"

"Harold—"

He pushed his way out the swinging door into the hall and through the living room. Omar, the cat, was at the door, sharpening his claws on the screen. Omar had only two claws—these had grown back after his declawing operation—and he used them with a special cleverness. He had even caught a mouse with them.

When Omar heard Harold coming he darted out of the way and hid under a chair. With pale yellow eyes he watched Harold pass. Then he came out, stretched, and went back into the kitchen.

Harold was bitterly disappointed. Celery was no substitute for a frozen candy bar. Frozen Mounds were his very favorites, too, either those or Hershey bars so melted you had to lick them off the wrapper.

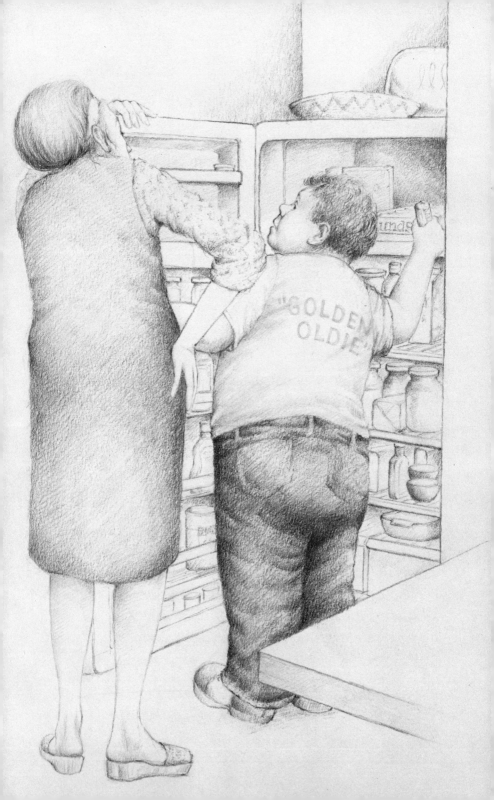

Harold's bicycle was leaning against the house, and he finished his celery, wiped his hands on his shirt, and slung one leg over the seat. He pedaled off slowly.

Harold had the best racing bicycle the local sports store had to offer. It had ten speeds, but Harold didn't need them. Harold always kept his bicycle in the lowest gear because it was easiest to pedal. The only time his bicycle got in a higher gear was when his knee accidentally struck the gear shift.

With his eyes on the street, he made his way to Ada's house and coasted down her driveway.

"Where's your friend?" he asked as he came to a stop.

"Figgy? Isn't he around front?"

"No."

"Well, where did he go? I was waiting here for him to come get the bicycle. Where is he?"

"I don't know."

"Hey, Figgy!" Ada rolled her bike up the driveway and stood looking up and down the street. She bit her bottom lip with her small pointed teeth. "Where did he go?"

"Beats me."

Harold and Ada stood at the edge of the street. Ada pushed her long black hair behind her ears. Harold rested on his bicycle, slumped over the handlebars.

Harold raised his eyes. "Well, I guess that's that."

He sighed. "What do you want to do now? We could ride over to my cousin's and see the new puppies. They're five of them and they're—"

"No. We are not going to your cousin's when Figgy's in trouble." She looked at him. "How would you feel if your grandfather was out there locked up in an empty cabin with a gun and your friends were casually going off to see some puppies?"

Harold blinked. His own grandfather owned a chain of three shoe stores so it was hard to imagine him being in that kind of trouble. Harold glanced down at his feet. The tricolored shoes he was wearing at this moment were a present from his grandfather. Harold said, "Well, I just thought . . ." He trailed off, then he said firmly, "I thought you'd be afraid to go without Figgy to show us the way. It's way out past Eastmont, you know."

"I'm not afraid of anything." Ada put her hair behind her ears. She shrugged. "Anyway, I'm not afraid of anything like that."

Harold nodded. He had even believed her first statement. He could not imagine Ada being afraid of anything. Period.

The first time he had seen Ada she had been eight years old, and she had very short black hair. She had been having a funeral for somebody's gerbil.

Harold could remember the occasion clearly. He

had come on the funeral unexpectedly. He had been walking home from his piano lesson and had gotten lost because his family had just moved into the neighborhood. There was a creek in the field behind his house, and as he was approaching the creek, he heard the sound of voices. He stepped into the clearing in time to see Ada preparing to launch a funeral barge.

He had stood there holding his piano book, "Pop Songs to Play and Sing," and watched. He had been impressed by the scene, by the two little girls with red swollen eyes, by Ada in complete control of the situation, by the tiny funeral barge that was an incredible craft made of ribbons and flowers and Popsicle sticks.

"We really ought to set fire to it," Ada was saying, "but I'm not sure it would burn." She looked up then and saw Harold.

The two sisters whose gerbil was about to be launched down the stream looked up at him too. Their eyes were so red they appeared to have on rosy, rimless glasses. They had been crying since the dead gerbil had been discovered that morning, and the only thing that had stopped their tears was their interest in Ada's imaginative arrangements.

"I was just passing through," he said to explain his intrusion. "Piano lesson." He held up his book, then rolled it and put it behind his back. Respectfully he stood like this while the funeral proceeded.

Afterward Ada had taken them all to her house. "You can come too," was how she had included him in the invitation, and he had gone along with them. She had showed them her stethoscope and let them listen to their hearts.

"I'm going to be a doctor, you know," she had told them.

The way she said it made Harold want to blurt out, "Oh, yeah, me too." But Harold knew he would never be a doctor. He did not want little children to burst into tears at the sight of him approaching with the black bag. WAAAAA! He did not want mothers to say to their children, "All right now, if you don't behave I'm going to take you to Dr. Harold V. Coleman this afternoon and have him give you a shot." WAAAAA! He imagined himself stiff and pale in his doctor's suit, waiting to vaccinate a screaming child. He imagined the mother saying, "Now, Ricky, it won't hurt at all. Dr. Harold will vaccinate himself first, won't you, Dr. Harold, to prove to little Ricky that it won't hurt?"

"What? What? Vaccinate myself?"

"Now, watch carefully, Ricky. Dr. Harold's going to vaccinate himself. Watch now. Go ahead, Dr. Harold, little Ricky's watching."

Then, to save face, he would actually have to vaccinate himself. WAAAAA!

On impulse he had said to Ada and the sisters, "I'm going to write books—comic books when I'm grown." They had all looked at him, right *at* him for the first time. The sisters' mouths were hanging open a little.

He sensed that he had their interest, and he became so filled with enthusiasm for this new occupation that he started a story then and there for one of his comic books. Stone Man was the main character, and Stone Man saved himself from bullets and other harm by turning himself to stone.

In this, the first and only episode, related that sunny day in Ada's living room, Stone Man found himself trapped in the sea. It was a desperate situation. The sisters' mouths hung open the whole time. Because Stone Man's fateful decision there at the bottom of the sea was whether he should turn to stone, and thereby sink and die, or be speared by the harpoons of the Sea Men and die that way.

When Harold was finished the sisters were silent for a few minutes and then in a rush made him promise, *promise* that he would mail them one of the first published Stone Man comic books.

"I promise," he had said solemnly. "You two will get the first copy."

"Let's get going, Harold," Ada said abruptly now. "We'll push our bikes over to the Boulevard through the field and then ride on through Eastmont."

"Right," he said, reluctantly putting aside Stone Man and the pleasant memory of the sisters' admiration. "Let's go."

They started walking, silently pushing their bikes through the grass. They passed into the field where there was an old chinaberry tree, and the tires of their bicycles popped the fallen berries.

"Keep up, Harold," Ada said.

"Right."

THE REAL TROUBLE

Slowly, awkwardly, Harold pedaled up the hill. Ahead of him Ada was making it look easy. She was seated while Harold was hunched over his handlebars, trying to go a few more yards before he had to get off and start pushing. He was conscious of the way he looked, like a demonstration of how *not* to ride a bicycle.

He thought that he and Ada could be part of a team that went around teaching people to ride bicycles. "This is the *right* way, folks," the announcer would say, and Ada would come sailing over the hill on her bicycle. "Note the ease with which she pedals. Note the straight back, the firm grip on the handlebars." There would be spontaneous applause as she flew past the admiring crowd.

"And now," the announcer would say, "now we

will see the *wrong* way." There would be a long pause. The crowd would grow restless. The announcer would consult his watch. He would say again, "And now we will see the *wrong* way."

Another silence and then he, Harold, would hove into view, puffing with effort, his face as red as a balloon.

"This, as you can see, is quite definitely the wrong way," the announcer would say. "How many of you agree with me?"

Every hand in the crowd would be raised, and Harold would pump by, hot and flushed beneath the arch of raised arms.

Harold's pedaling grew harder. He stopped and got off his bicycle. He started pushing it up the hill. Ahead of him Ada was still riding, apparently effortlessly.

"Hey, wait up," he called.

Ada turned, saw him, and got off her bicycle. "What's wrong?"

"Nothing," he said. Then he added as he got closer, "This bicycle slows me up."

"I thought that bicycle had about ten speeds."

"It does." He sighed. "It's got ten speeds all right— Pedal, Pedal Harder, Pedal Real Hard, Pedal Standing Up, Pedal Bending Over . . ." He joined her and stood for a moment, breathing hard. "That's work."

She smiled slightly, showing her pointed teeth. "Well, we better keep going."

"Yeah, sure."

Slowly they pushed their bikes up the hill. They were now on the new highway, and they had all four lanes to themselves. Harold thought it would be pleasant to have all this space if only Ada had not been in such a hurry to get to Figgy's grandfather.

As they walked Harold said suddenly, "I guess you know what my real trouble is."

Ada said, "No." She didn't look at him. "What is the trouble?"

"Well, the real trouble, if you want to know, is that I'm weak from lack of food. My mom's got me on a diet." It was the first time he had admitted this to anybody. He felt better just to have it out in the open.

"A diet?"

"Yeah, she says I'm too fat." He felt unburdened. He had been carrying excess fat around for years, and no one had ever commented on it. No one had called him Fat Harold or Pig V. Coleman. No one had teased him. In fact, the only person he could remember commenting on his size was the clerk in the boys' department of Belk's who always said, "The husky sizes are right this way," as soon as he came in with his mom.

Still, Harold had always felt the thought was there, and now it was a relief to have his disability put into words.

Ada glanced at him. "I never think of you as being fat."

"You don't?" He looked at her closely to see if there was any chance she was putting him on. Then he said, "The truth is that I've always been fat. I was fat when I was born. I was fat in the stroller, fat in the sandbox, a pumpkin in the nursery school play. One time I was even a hippopotamus." He broke off and glanced around. "Hey, how much farther do you think the cabin is?"

"I don't know."

"I wish I knew." It was important to Harold that he assess his strength at this point and see if he was going to be equal to the task. By ten o'clock he would like to be home in front of the television eating, if possible, some diet popcorn.

He glanced at Ada, but she was looking ahead at the long white highway. "Sometimes things make me sad."

Harold thought instantly of the frozen Mound. "Me, too," he said sincerely. Then after a moment he cleared his throat and said, "What's made you sad?" He knew it was bound to be more than candy bars.

"Oh." She shook her head. "Just Figgy."

"Yeah," he said. He felt a sudden stab of guilt. "Well, he's made me sad too." He waited to see if she was going to add anything more. She wasn't.

"Figgy is in a very sad situation," he said for emphasis. "The Goat Man too."

Still Harold was puzzled. He did not understand why the Goat Man was making such a fuss. People had to move all the time. Jobs changed. Highways changed. You had to be ready to change too. It was the way life was.

He himself had not particularly wanted to move into this neighborhood either, but he had done it. He hadn't locked himself in his room and refused to come out. Well, actually he had done that, he remembered, but as soon as his mother called, "Har-old! Piz-za!" he had come out in good spirits. He hadn't sulked.

And then, as he remembered it, he had come running downstairs to the very smallest piece of pizza he had ever seen. It couldn't have been more than an inch wide.

That was the kind of thing his mother was famous for, he thought. "Har-old! Pop-corn!" He would use up about a thousand calories running into the house for the treat, and there would be one unbuttered piece of popcorn on a platter.

Or she would wait until he was miles away to make him run as far as possible. "Har-old! Can-dy!"

"Coming, I'm coming." His feet would fly over the ground. He would go *through* the screen door. "Where's the candy? Where is it? Where's the candy?"

"There."

"Where? I don't see it. Where?"

"There. Right *there*. The M and M."

The M and M! *The* M and M! *One* M and M!

"You call *one* M and M candy?" He would want to protest by refusing it, but he never could. One M and M was better than nothing if you let it melt very slowly.

He glanced over at Ada and she looked as serious as ever. He said, "Figgy will be all right. I know he will. And so will the Goat Man."

"I hope so."

AN ACCIDENT

Figgy was taking the long way home because it was the only way he knew. He had stopped running now and was walking. He walked slowly, thinking about his discomforts. He was hungry, he was tired, he was cold, and his feet hurt.

Then abruptly he stopped thinking about these things, and his mind turned to his mother. He had not thought about her for a long time, but then it had been a long time since he had been this lonely.

All Figgy remembered of his mother was that one time she had ridden a black cow. He didn't remember where and he didn't remember when. He was not even sure he had been there. He might have just heard about it. But whenever he thought about his mother he thought of a woman with brown hair and brown eyes and brown freckles riding on a big black cow through a soft green field. Those were the only colors in the memory.

Once when he had been at his Aunt Bena's he had said, "My mom used to ride a black cow."

Aunt Bena had turned to him, smiling. "Where on earth did you get that idea? Why, Fiona wouldn't come within ten feet of a cow."

"Yes," he had said, "she used to ride a black cow, or one time she did anyway."

"I knew your mom better than you did, and I can tell you she never was on any black cow."

Figgy had not answered, but he wondered about it sometimes—how he could be the only person in the world who knew his mother had ridden a cow. Anyway he was glad he did know because it was a nice thing to remember about your mother.

It was still daylight when Figgy got to the new highway, and he felt better for a while. Having a whole superhighway to himself was a good feeling. He walked down the middle of the highway, holding onto his rabbit's foot.

He had walked about a half mile when he heard a shout behind him. He turned quickly. Ada was just coming over the crest of the hill on her bicycle.

"Hey, wait!" she shouted. "Hey, Figgy!" She rode quickly down the hill and came to a screeching halt beside him, leaving her tire marks on the white pave-

ment. Then she stood with one foot on the ground. "What happened to you?"

Figgy shrugged. "I don't know."

"I mean, we came out and you were gone—vanished."

Figgy shrugged again.

"Didn't you think we were coming?"

"I don't know."

All his life Figgy had been answering questions with, "I don't know." His teachers had gotten the answer for hard questions like, "Well, Figgy, why do *you* think you aren't doing well in math?"

"I don't know."

His grandfather had gotten the answer for hard questions like, "What did you do *that* for?"

"I don't know." Sometimes it seemed to Figgy there were nothing *but* hard questions.

Ada asked again, "But why did you leave?"

"I don't know."

Harold came over the crest of the hill then. He was walking, pushing his bike. He got on and coasted down to where they were standing. "What'd you go running off for?" he asked Figgy when he stopped.

"He doesn't know," Ada said. "I guess he was worried about his grandfather and wanted to get there and we were taking so long about everything."

Figgy nodded quickly.

"Well, how much farther is it?" Harold asked.

"It's not far, just over there. That's the grocery store where we used to buy stuff."

"Well, let's get going," Harold said. "You can ride with one of us."

Figgy hesitated. He looked from Ada to Harold. He did not want to ride on either bicycle. He said, "I'll just run along beside you guys."

"No," Harold said firmly, "You couldn't keep up. Now, get on, one or the other. It's getting dark and I want to get there."

Still Figgy hesitated. He remembered how Ada had come over the crest of the hill. He thought of her speed, how her hair had flowed behind her like a banner. He glanced down at the black marks her tires had left on the concrete. Then he remembered how slowly Harold had come into view. Harold had actually been walking, pushing his bicycle.

"I'll go with you," Figgy said to Harold.

"Well, get on. I want to get there before dark." As Harold said this he realized the truth of it. The old cabin, the old man inside with a gun. Add to that a dark night—there would probably be no moon—the thought was enough to make the soul shudder. He decided that before they approached the cabin he was going to make Figgy call out their identities in a good loud voice. Especially, "This big boy is Harold V. Coleman, one of my special friends."

Harold thought he would take one step forward,

bow slightly, and give the peace sign with both hands.

He remembered suddenly the pictures of the Goat Man he had seen in the newspaper. The Goat Man was a grim old man, bitter. His mouth was as straight a line as you could draw with a ruler. His eyes were pieces of iron. Harold decided that he did not want to meet the Goat Man at all.

He said, "Get on the bicycle, will you!" to Figgy. His reluctance made his voice unusually harsh. "We haven't got all day."

Slowly Figgy climbed on the seat of the bicycle and held onto Harold's waist. He was torn between the desire to hold on with both hands and the need to hold the rabbit's foot.

"Don't go too fast," Figgy said.

"Are you kidding? With the two of us on here, we'll be lucky to go at all. Just hold on and be quiet."

"That's what I was doing."

"And don't stretch my T-shirt."

Slowly Harold pushed off and coasted down the hill, his hand on the brakes. He had the feeling that something was going to go wrong. He realized that he had had this feeling all along, ever since he and Ada had started out. Now, as the shadows on the white road lengthened, the feeling grew.

They reached the bottom of the hill and, pedaling furiously, Harold managed to get almost halfway up the next hill before slowing down. Then he snaked his way back and forth across the highway, going another hundred yards before he stopped. "You'll have to walk the rest of the way," Harold said.

"Oh, well, sure," Figgy said, getting off quickly. "That wasn't so bad."

Ahead of them Ada was still managing to ride. She was pedaling sitting down.

"Has she got a motor on that or something?" Figgy asked admiringly.

"No."

"She can really ride."

"I know." Harold took this as a criticism of his own riding, and he walked faster. At the top of the hill he said sharply, "Get on," and waited while Figgy climbed on the back.

"Hey, look where Ada is," Figgy said as he got settled.

"I see her."

Harold pushed off awkwardly and began to coast down the hill. He could feel Figgy's hands at his waist.

He began to pedal. He was ashamed that Ada was so far ahead. She was almost at the top of the second hill now. He pedaled faster. He could feel Figgy's hands tighten at his waist. They were like claws. "You're pinching," he said over his shoulder.

The bicycle was now going a little faster than Harold intended.

"Slow down," Figgy wailed. Figgy's mind often

worked on instinct, like an animal's. He could sense approaching storms and other natural disasters, and he sensed danger now. He could almost smell it.

He grabbed his rabbit's foot and held it tightly against his chest. He wailed, "Slow down," again to Harold's back.

Harold applied the brakes. There was a little sand on the road and the front wheel skidded and pulled sharply to the left. Harold let out his breath in a hissing sound. It was like air going out of a tire. Figgy was too frightened to make any sound at all. He held his rabbit's foot tighter and shut his eyes. His mind closed like a fist.

The bike moved jerkily. It was going too fast, despite the fact that Harold was applying the brakes, and it was swerving toward the side of the road. Harold didn't know what was happening. It was as if the bicycle had suddenly gotten a will of its own.

"Hold on!" he gasped to Figgy, and at that moment the bicycle went off the road.

The front wheel flew up into the air, and then the bicycle went over the hill in a wide arc. Harold went with the bicycle, and a tangled mass of boy and wheels ground-looped down the dirt hill and came to a stop in a cloud of reddish dust.

Figgy fell off backward as soon as they left the road. He twisted in the air and then landed hard on the side of the road, his head on the pavement.

The whole thing had taken only six seconds, but now Harold lay under the bicycle, looking up through the rear wheel. He didn't know what had happened.

Looking up at the sky through the spinning wheel gave him a weird feeling. It was as if he were looking at dozens of little wedge-shaped mirrors, in which the sky was reflected. He was dizzy. He thought suddenly of a glass ball that hung from the ceiling of the old movie theater and reflected everything in tiny cubes. It would make you sick if you watched it long enough.

He didn't know he was looking through the bicycle wheel, not even when the wheel began to slow down. Finally it stopped and Harold saw that he was looking up through the wires.

Behind him, Figgy was lying with his eyes closed. Neither of them moved.

1/3,348,000,000

The accident had been almost silent, and Ada heard nothing. She was at the top of the next hill when she stopped and glanced back. All she saw was the empty stretch of highway. She stood without moving, wondering where Harold and Figgy were.

"Harold! Figgy!"

She put her hair behind her ears. "Where did they go?" She mouthed the words. Just then she saw, about halfway up the hill, Figgy's body. It lay on one side of the road like a doll. Her eyes traveled down the bank by the highway and she saw Harold twisted in his bicycle.

For a moment Ada had a hard time associating those two bodies with her two friends. Her eyes took in the sight, but her mind was still pretending to wonder where Harold and Figgy were.

Then she knew, and her head felt suddenly heavy. "Oh, no." Her blood began to pound in her throat. She kept looking at the two bodies until they blurred. Then with a kind of desperate twisting movement she turned and looked at the green hills, at the peaceful white roads, at the fields. There was not a sound anywhere. It was impossible to believe, looking at those peaceful hills, what had happened.

She looked back at Figgy and Harold. She had a terrible dread of going closer. She waited a moment, holding tightly to her bicycle, to see if either of the bodies was going to move.

"Harold! Figgy!"

There was no answer. She set her bicycle down and began running down the hill toward Figgy and Harold. As she ran, the strength came back into her body. She began to run faster.

As she came up the hill she decided that Harold looked the worse and she slid down the hill to where he was lying. She looked down at him through the bicycle wheel.

"Are you all right?"

Harold looked back. He didn't know what had happened. He felt weird. He thought he was in a small wire cage, and Ada was staring at him.

"Harold, are you all right?"

His eyes focused, and for the first time he became aware of where he was. He saw Ada. Gradually he realized there was not one single part of him that didn't hurt.

"Can you move?" Ada asked. "Are you all right?"

"I don't know whether I'm all right or not," he said through dry lips.

"I'll try to lift the bicycle."

"Be careful."

Slowly she unwrapped him from the bicycle, and the bicycle went sliding on down the hill. Harold sat up. He felt dazed, a little sick. "I must have been unconscious," he said.

"Can you move?"

"Yeah, I can move. I'm all right." He held out his hands. "I'm fine. I was just knocked unconscious." There was a kind of wonder in his voice. His first unconsciousness.

"Can you get up?"

"Well, I can try." He got up slowly, hunched over his knees. "Nothing's broken." He got to his feet. It seemed impossible after the kind of fall he had taken that his bones weren't crushed, but it was true. He imagined that this was because his bones were well-wrapped in fat. Good packing. There was that advantage in being fat anyway. He imagined a bumper sticker put out by the American Medical Association. "Wrap your bones in a protective covering—fat!" He imagined himself in a magazine advertisement, standing fat and solid in the shallow end of the swimming pool. "I protect valuable bones and organs with an inexpensive and easily manufactured layer of fat."

"We better see about Figgy," Ada said.

Up until that second Harold had forgotten Figgy. He turned quickly and watched Ada scamper up the hill. He could barely see Figgy at the top, but he could see that Figgy was not moving.

Harold started up the hill too, taking it slow. He began dusting off his clothes. He went over and stood behind Ada, still unconsciously brushing off his pants. All his breath eased out of him as he looked at Figgy.

Figgy lay as he had fallen. He was on his back, his arms and legs spread out straight except for one leg that was bent the wrong way at the knee. His eyes were closed. His mouth was open. In one hand, lying loosely as if it were on display, was the rabbit's foot.

"Oh," Harold said in a low mournful way.

Ada knelt and put one hand on Figgy's chest.

Harold said, "Oh," again as if he were tired. All his life Harold had avoided sights like this. He did not like to see people who were hurt. He sometimes thought this was the main difference between him and everybody else in the world. He thought of him-

self and the rest of the world as a great fraction—
1/3,348,000,000.

He was just different, that was all. When the rest
of the world was rushing to fires and accidents, risk-
ing accidents themselves in order to get there in time
to see the disaster, he was turning and going staunchly
in the opposite direction. He didn't *want* to see hurt
people.

Once at the beach he had stood in the warm sand
and almost fainted while hundreds of people ran past
him on their way to see a drowned man who had just
been pulled from the ocean. How could people stand
it? he wondered. He felt, looking at Figgy, that his
own soul was seeping out of his body.

"Is he dead?" he asked finally, choking a little on
the last word. It was a hard word to say in a situation
like this. He remembered how when his dog Sammy
had been put to sleep by the vet, Harold had said
harshly, "We had the vet *kill* him." And his mother
had said, "No, no, Harold, we had him put to *sleep*."
He understood now why she had put it that way.

He realized he had spoken so softly that Ada hadn't
heard him. He asked again, "Is he dead?"

"No," Ada said.

"Are you sure?"

"He's *not* dead."

"Well, that's a relief." Suddenly Harold wanted to

say, "It's my fault," but he felt that might be asking for sympathy, as if he wanted Ada to turn and say, "Don't be silly. You couldn't help it." That was exactly what he did want her to say, but he knew he didn't deserve it. It *was* his fault. Period.

He stood there, silent and miserable, not wanting to look at Figgy, not able to look away. He felt large and useless, like one of those huge gas-filled figures in the Christmas parade.

FIGGY

"Figgy! Figgy, can you hear me?" Ada asked. She took his hand and patted it. "Figgy!"

Figgy heard his name, but it seemed that he was being called from a great distance. The voice got farther away and then closer. *"Figgy!"* Someone was touching him, but somehow he was being touched from a great distance too.

"Figgy, can you hear me?"

Figgy felt a warm hand on his forehead and suddenly he knew everything. He had been in an accident. He was lying beside the road hurt worse than he had ever been hurt in his life. He might even be dying.

He moaned at the thought and Ada said quickly, "Figgy, come on, Figgy, open your eyes."

That was the one thing Figgy did not want to do. As long as he did not *see* the hurt, then it might go away. There was always hope until you looked. Once you saw the hurt, then it was real. He moaned.

"Figgy, try to open your eyes. Look at me."

In his misery Figgy squeezed his eyes shut tighter. He felt as cold as if snow had fallen on him. He thought that if snow fell all at once, instead of flake by flake, it would feel like this.

He wondered suddenly if the world was somehow protesting his injury by turning the summer to winter. Maybe the world really did care. Maybe snow *had* fallen.

Then he felt how solid the earth was beneath him. He felt the clouds moving across the sky above him. He imagined the trees and the hills. It seemed to Figgy then that the earth was the most powerful thing there was. It kept going. No matter what happened. And no matter who it happened to.

"Figgy, open your eyes if you can."

Figgy moaned again. One summer he had been at his Aunt Bena's, and the thing he remembered most about that summer was his aunt's wonderful generosity.

He would say, "Aunt Bena, can I have a quarter? Please just let me have *one quarter*."

"A quarter! What do you want a quarter for? You think I'm made of money?"

He would beg and beg, but she would be as hard and firm as a banker. "Absolutely not! No quarter!"

And then, just as Figgy would give up and start from the room, she would turn generous. It was wonderful the way she did it, Figgy thought, because she always waited until he really had given up hope. "Oh, here," she would say, "take the quarter," and toss it to him.

Now as he lay there hurt and scared, he wanted the world to turn generous in the same way. Now that he was leaving the room—maybe he really was dying—he wanted the world to cry, "Oh, here, Figgy, here," and toss to him the perfectly good body he had had only an hour before.

Ada said sternly, "Figgy, open your eyes. I know you can hear me."

Figgy still did not want to do that. He wanted to give the world time. At Aunt Bena's he always walked to the door very slowly, giving her every chance. Once he opened his eyes . . .

Ada lifted one of his eyelids and Figgy sighed and opened both eyes. It was all over now, he thought. The hurt was real.

Ada said, "Figgy, you've had an accident."

"I know." Tears began to roll down his cheeks.

"Is he all right?" Harold asked.

Figgy looked up at Harold. He said, "I'm sick."

Figgy spoke so quietly that Harold couldn't hear

him. "What did he say?" He was bending over Figgy now too, casting a shadow on him. Urgently he asked it again. "What did you say?"

"He says he feels sick," Ada repeated. "Now, Figgy, just lie still, hear, and you're going to be all right."

"Where's my rabbit's foot?" Figgy asked. He strained to raise himself up and look around.

"It's there in your hand," Harold said. He leaned down and closed Figgy's fingers around the rabbit's foot. Figgy sighed as he felt the soft fur.

"Now lie still," Ada said.

"Yes, one of the first rules of accidents is not to move around," Harold said.

"I feel sick."

"I know," Ada said. "Your leg's broken, Figgy. You're going to be all right, but your leg—it's the right one—will have to be in a cast for a while."

"I really don't feel good."

"I know. Just lie still and we're going to get help."

"And I'm cold."

"Here's my sweater." Ada took it off and covered him in one movement. "Give me your T-shirt, Harold."

"My T-shirt?"

"Yes, and hurry."

Harold pulled his T-shirt off over his head and spread it on top of Figgy. "It's my Golden Oldie T-shirt," he said. The bold black call letters of the radio station made Figgy's face seem faded and blurred.

"Is that better, Figgy?" Ada asked.

Figgy nodded. He began to rub his thumb back and forth over his rabbit's foot. Then he looked up at Ada and said, "I want my grandfather."

"We'll—"

"I want my *grandfather*," he said louder. In that moment he saw his grandfather as having the same kind of strength that the world had. His grandfather was unchanging. He was all-powerful. He was not a person who turned this way and that with the wind. Aunt Bena's generosity suddenly seemed human; his granfather's was more like nature, like a stream. His grandfather was the only person who could make things all right now.

He tried to raise himself up. He struggled with Ada. He said, *"I want my grandfather."*

"We'll get him." Ada pressed him back. She tucked the sweater firmly around his neck. "We'll get your grandfather right now."

THE EXTRA
HIPPOPOTAMUS

Behind Ada, Harold stood motionless. Without his shirt he felt unprotected and vulnerable. His body sometimes seemed to him to be magnetized to danger. If a rock was thrown or an arrow shot, if a limb fell or a bee flew, it would come as if drawn by a magnet right to his body. Unclothed, his body was even more vulnerable. He crossed his arms over his chest.

"We'll get your grandfather right now," Ada said again. "Just *lie still*."

Harold stood silently staring at the back of Ada's head. Her long hair was spread over her shoulders like a cape.

He cleared his throat and said, "Well, I better do that—go get his grandfather." He paused. He hoped

for a moment that Ada would say, "No, you can't go by yourself."

Ada said, "Yes, go on."

"Right."

She glanced at him over her shoulder. "And hurry, Harold."

"Right."

He turned and began walking away from Ada and Figgy. The only sound was that of his pants' legs brushing together as he walked.

He had a sudden desire to turn and walk backward, the way he used to do when he was little and reluctant to leave somebody or someplace. One time he had walked backward for two blocks when he had to leave a birthday party before the refreshments. He couldn't see the party—it was going on inside the house in the rec room—but he kept watching the house until he had to turn the corner.

Now he would not let himself even glance back. He kept walking quickly and purposefully up the hill. He stepped around Ada's fallen bicycle and went around the bend. He kept walking.

His head was bowed. His eyes were on his feet. Strangely enough it was himself he felt sorry for and not Figgy.

As he walked he remembered a play his Bible school had put on the summer he was six. It had been a

Noah's ark production, and the children had been put in pairs, representing different animals. They were to come out on the stage in twos, say verses, and go into the ark. Harold had been absent a lot during Bible school because of a sore throat, so when he arrived the day before the play, there was nothing left for him to be. All the animals had been taken. The pairs had been made.

Finally in desperation the teacher had said, "All right, Harold, you can be an extra hippopotamus."

He couldn't believe what he had heard. An extra hippopotamus! He had stood there, and in his mind the pale green Sunday school room had become a jungle. The stage had become an ark. Billy Boyeland had become Noah.

And then Noah had stood up and thundered, "Now remember what I said—two by two. All right, everybody in the ark."

A pause while the animals shuffled and pushed and slid into line. Then Noah cried, "Hey, wait a minute. Who are you?"

"Me? I'm the extra hippopotamus."

"The *extra* hippopotamus! Who needs an *extra* hippopotamus? Step out of line."

"But—"

"Out! All right now, let's get moving. Someone shove the extra hippopotamus out of the way."

The thought was more than Harold could bear. "Did you say for me to be the *extra hippopotamus,* Miss Cole?" He was amazed that his voice sounded normal.

"Yes, get over there with Brenda and Cindy."

"Miss Cole, I can't be the *extra hippopotamus.*"

"Brenda, you and Cindy move over. Make room for Harold."

"But, *Miss Cole*—"

"It's settled, Harold."

It all came back to him now as he walked down the highway by himself. He had dreamed about the situation a lot that summer. In his dreams all the other animals had clomped happily into the ark. The heavy wooden door had slammed shut. The extra hippopotamus had been left alone.

Then the extra hippopotamus had turned and walked all by himself through the world until the rains started and the floods came. Then he had climbed up on the tallest hill and stood all by himself and watched the noisy ark float away, bobbing happily on the waves.

The idea had haunted Harold during that sixth summer. He could not even think of the extra hippopotamus without tears coming to his eyes. And now, even though it had been long forgotten, the thought rose to haunt him again.

It was, he thought, one of those ideas that keep popping up. He would probably forget it now, and later, when he was forty or fifty, driving down a highway some dark night, the extra hippopotamus would float into his mind like an old forgotten song.

He came to the end of the paving, and he walked along on the gravel, then on the graded dirt. He passed huge tractors and graders and trucks that had been parked for the night. He passed stacks of black pipes and piles of gravel. It made him feel even lonelier somehow.

He came to the end of the grading, and ahead was the cleared land. Harold picked his way slowly over the soft ribbed earth. He stepped carefully around the ferns that had started shooting up out of the newly turned ground.

Still Harold's mind was on the extra hippopotamus. He went around a grove of trees and skirted a large pile of gray rocks. Then he paused and glanced up. Right then everything went out of his mind but the Goat Man.

Because ahead was the Goat Man's cabin. It sat stark and alone in the middle of the clearing except for a large pile of roots and logs that had been piled to the right. The cabin itself seemed little more than a pile of trash nailed together. Harold thought it was like a before-and-after picture. Turn this pile of trash into this neat *house* of trash in your spare time. A re-cycled home.

Harold wondered again what all the fuss was about. Slowly he approached the cabin. He had hoped on the long walk that he would find the cabin surrounded by reporters with cameras and policemen with guns. Harold would walk up to one of them and blurt out the bad news. Then one of the policemen could con-tact the Goat Man through a loudspeaker.

"Mr. Gryshevich, your grandson has been injured. Come out with your hands over your head."

That was the way it would have happened in the movies. In real life it was going to be different, Harold could see that. All the workmen had gone home and were eating supper. The deputy sheriff was probably watching *I Love Lucy* on the television. Harold was going to have to go up to the cabin alone, knock at the door, and wait for the door to be opened.

As he came slowly down the incline, Harold thought he knew exactly how the Goat Man's eyes would look, staring at him above the double barrel of his shotgun. Harold felt goose bumps rise on his arms. He wished he had his shirt.

He thought of himself in a magazine advertisement, standing on a large empty battlefield. "Whenever I go out to meet danger, I shield myself with a light protec-tive covering of goose bumps." It didn't seem enough.

YOU AND ME AND A DOUBLE-BARRELED SHOTGUN

The ground was still rough because it would not be graded properly until all the trash was removed. Harold picked his way across the bare, uneven ground. Above him the woods had been so thinned that they were transparent. He could see the setting sun.

Harold glanced at the cabin again. In that moment, with the dark shadows upon it, Harold suddenly found he could imagine what the cabin had looked like before the bulldozers came. The trees would have grown right to the edge of the cabin, making a wall of shade. In the cool thick trees the cabin would not have looked so trashy. The worn wood, the scuffed porch boards, the makeshift roof—the trees would have made them all right.

The last light of day hung over the land, and the wide path cleared for the new highway suddenly had the look, to Harold, not of planned engineering but of nature gone wild. It looked, Harold thought, as if a tornado or freak wind had come ripping through the forest and up the valley, a wind strong enough to sweep the land clean, to part the forest. It did not, at this moment, seem anything like progress.

Harold paused. "Mr. Gryshevich!"

He waited but there was no answer. He tried to imagine Mr. Gryshevich there in front of the cabin with his goats. He tried to imagine Mr. Gryshevich sitting on the edge of the porch, scratching the goats' heads. It was important for him to get this picture, to turn back the clock and see what Mr. Gryshevich had been like before the bulldozers came. But the picture wouldn't come clear. The only sign that anybody had ever lived here was an old thermometer nailed by the door with a Coca-Cola bottle opener beneath.

"Mr. Gryshevich!"

Harold was watching the door of the cabin, and he thought that it opened a little. He waited to see if he could catch sight of that glint of steel he was always hearing about. The gun barrel. He thought of how he must look standing there, fat and pale and scared. The perfect target.

He took a few steps forward. The ground was soft

and fertile. It was right for planting. Harold stepped in front of the pile of trash.

"Mr. Gryshevich!"

He was directly in front of the cabin, and he stood for a moment looking at it. The work on the cabin showed now, the way the work showed in an old patchwork quilt his great-grandmother had made.

Harold kept looking at the cabin. He had seen a million houses and buildings, but he had never seen one, not even the Empire State Building, that showed work the way this cabin did. Not a piece of this cabin had been bought new in the lumber yard. It had been found or cut down or dragged through the forest. It looked better suddenly to Harold than buildings made by men in yellow hard hats.

"Mr. Gryshevich!" Harold called again.

He paused. There was no sign that he had been heard, but Harold had the feeling that he had been. Suddenly, as if he had X-ray eyes, he saw beyond the walls of the cabin. Time rolled back for a moment and he saw Mr. Gryshevich inside his house, in front of the fire. He saw the goats, Brownie and Pepper, and the trees and everything the way it had been.

"Mr. Gryshevich, I am Harold V. Coleman," he said in a loud, clear voice. "I am a friend of Figgy's." He paused, swallowed. This was the hard part. "Figgy has had an accident."

Harold slumped because as soon as he said that it became the present again. He caught his breath because he could see now that the door was opening. Harold waited for the glint of steel. The shotgun. He had never looked into the barrel of one of those before. He had never looked into eyes like the Goat Man's before either. He didn't know which was going to be worse.

The door opened slowly, as if it were heavy. Harold swallowed. He took another step forward in his tri-colored shoes.

"Mr. Gryshevich," he said again, "Figgy has had an accident. His leg is broken, the right leg."

The door was still opening. It was slow motion. Harold couldn't see anything in the doorway, though. It was only a widening space.

"Mr. Gryshevich, it was really my fault, the accident." Harold thought he might as well get the whole thing out in the open. "He was riding on the back of my bicycle and I was going too fast. We wrecked."

Suddenly Harold shut his eyes because that old man coming out of the door seemed a very personal, private thing, like birth. For the first time it was clear to Harold what the value of something could be to the man who had made it.

Harold sighed and opened his eyes. The Goat Man was on the porch now, looking toward Harold.

The shadows had deepened and the porch was dark. Harold could not see the Goat Man's face, but the man's shape, big and solid, bent forward like an old tree, moved through the dusk to the edge of the steps where there was more light.

They looked at each other then across the ruined land, the fat boy and the old man.

It was not at all the way Harold had thought it would be. There was nothing to be afraid of. Instead he felt run through with sadness. He who had avoided looking at hurt people all his life was now looking right into the eyes of a man who had been mortally wounded.

With great kindness in his voice Harold said, "I've come to take you to Figgy."

The Goat Man didn't say anything, just nodded his head as if he were ducking a low beam and stepped off the porch. He was exactly as he had appeared in the Sunday newspaper pictures, Harold thought—craggy, tough, a face like granite.

Harold stood and waited for him. Then they began to walk away from the cabin together.

It seemed a touching moment to Harold—the old man leaving the cabin without looking back, especially now that he knew what life was going to be like in another house. To take the Goat Man's mind off these painful thoughts, Harold said, "Let me tell you about the accident."

He hesitated for a moment, going over it in his mind. He glanced at the Goat Man's profile. It was strong enough to be carved on a mountain.

"Well," he said, "it started the other day when Ada, this girl, and I were getting ready to play Monopoly." And then he went on, careful not to spare himself, and told the Goat Man all that had happened.

AND NO
NURSE EITHER

Ada was still kneeling by Figgy. She kept glancing up every now and then to see if Harold and Figgy's grandfather were coming. "How do you feel now?"

"My leg's starting to hurt."

"I know, but how do you feel other than that?"

"I don't know."

"Can you move this leg?"

"Yes, I can move everything." He paused. Tears came to his eyes, spilled over, and rolled back into his hair. "Only I don't feel like it."

"I know."

He really began to cry then. He turned his head to the side and said, "Who invented the old bicycle anyway?"

"Listen, you're going to be all right," Ada said. "We'll get my dad—he's a doctor—and he'll put your leg in a cast and—"

"I don't want any doctor fixing my leg," Figgy said. Then, anticipating her next suggestion, he said quickly, "And no nurse either!" The only medical person he had ever come in contact with was a nurse who came to his school on Wednesdays.

"But, Figgy, this doctor is my *father*. He fixes people's arms and legs all the time." She wiped his tears away with the edge of Harold's T-shirt. Then, seeing how much dirt came off on the shirt, she began gently to wipe the rest of his face. "One time I fell out of a tree—I was five—and I broke my arm and my father put a cast on it and—"

"No."

"Figgy—"

"My *grandfather* will set it. Nobody's touching me but my *grandfather*."

"Figgy—"

"*NO!*"

"All right, all right," Ada said. She began to wipe his face again. It was all she knew to do. After a moment she said, "We can play Monopoly while you're getting better."

"What?" He opened his eyes and looked at her.

"We can play Monopoly."

"Monopoly?"

"Yes."

"But I won't be able to come over," he said. His voice broke and the tears started again. "My leg will be in a cast."

"But you can keep the game at *your* house and then Harold and I will come over and play with *you*. From now on it will be your game."

"Oh." Figgy closed his eyes, and the piles of crisp green and pink and yellow money drifted into his mind. He thought of the tiny metal shoe and the ship and the thimble. He thought of Boardwalk. He imagined the satisfaction of red hotels on the rich blue, of saying, "Boardwalk, that's mine. Let's see, that will be two thousand dollars, please."

Ada kept wiping his face. She said, "Someday, Figgy, I'm going to be a doctor, and then I'll be able to set people's legs. Would you mind *me* setting your leg?"

"Yes."

"Not if I was a doctor you wouldn't."

"Yes, I would."

Eyes closed, Figgy let his mind wander back to the Monopoly game.

Suddenly Ada stopped wiping his face and said, "Oh, here they come, Figgy. At last! Here comes your grandfather."

Figgy leaned up on one elbow and looked at his grandfather coming over the crest of the hill. For Figgy, it was like seeing the sun rise.

"Grandpa!" He waved his free hand in the air. "Grandpa, it's me, Figgy! I'm over here!"

Figgy waited a moment and then turned to Ada and said, "He sees me but he won't wave." He lay back down. He looked up at the sky and sighed. He was warm now. He smiled. "I knew he would come."

"I did too, Figgy."

Figgy lay there for a moment and then he raised himself up and looked to see where his grandfather was now. He beckoned to his grandfather to hurry. "Come on, Grandpa," he called.

His grandfather kept walking at the same pace. Figgy had never seen his grandfather walk any faster or any slower than this. For some reason, he was glad his grandfather didn't start running.

He watched while his grandfather paused long enough for Harold to pick up Ada's bicycle. Then they started walking again.

As they got closer Ada stood up and brushed off her clothes. She said, "Hi," and stepped back.

"My leg's broken, Grandpa," Figgy said. His voice cracked on the words.

He started crying again. It was the generosity of the world that was making him cry this time. "Here, Figgy, here's your grandfather."

Quickly Figgy wiped his tears away. As his grand-father knelt beside him, he said bravely, "Except for my leg, I'm fine."

His grandfather gently put his hand on Figgy's leg. No doctor could make you feel better just by touching you, Figgy thought. Only his grandfather had that power.

Figgy said, "If it's got to be set, I want you to do it. I don't want any doctor." Then he added quickly, "And no nurse either!" Figgy glanced over at Ada and Harold, who were standing together. "My grandpa has set animals' legs hundreds of times."

His grandfather shook his head and Figgy said, "Well, you've done it *some* times. I know that."

In the pause that followed Harold cleared his throat and said, "Sir, there's probably a phone at that grocery store back there. I'll be glad to go make the call, to summon an ambulance and a doctor, if you want me to."

"Get my dad," Ada said.

Harold nodded. He waited and then said again, "I'll be glad to make the call. Her father's a doctor."

The Goat Man nodded. Harold glanced at Ada and said, "You want to come with me or just wait?"

"I'll wait."

"I'll be right back."

MR. GRYSHEVICH AND
HAROLD V. COLEMAN

For a moment, though, Harold kept standing there. He watched Figgy and the Goat Man.

It was funny. Harold felt sorry for Figgy lying there with a broken leg, but he did not really know how Figgy felt. Harold had never broken a leg. He knew it must be painful, but still he could not imagine how it felt to lie there on the white, white pavement and not be allowed to move.

Harold took a deep breath. It had always been hard for him to know how other people felt. He remembered that he had not known how Ada felt when her mother was dying, even though he had been closer to her that summer than anybody else. She had said to him over and over, "You are the only person I can be with this summer."

He remembered he had sat out in her back yard for days helping her look for four-leaf clovers. They had found seven of them and Ada had made them into a little wreath and pressed it in a book. Every time Harold had found one of those clovers, he had felt as if he were really helping Ada's mother. He imagined her getting better and better.

They had been sitting in the yard when Aunt Margaret came out and asked Ada to come in the house because her father wanted to talk to her. Ada had looked at Harold then and said, "My mother's dead. I know it."

Harold had been looking right into her eyes at that moment. He had said, "She couldn't be." The little wreath of clovers turned to dust in his mind.

"I *know* it."

Ada had kept looking at him for a moment, and there had been something different about her. Something had changed for Ada, and Harold could see it in her eyes or in her mouth. Her face looked smaller, or something. Before he could put his finger on exactly what was different, she had gotten up and gone into the house.

Harold had kept sitting there by the bird feeder until Aunt Margaret came back outside. She said, "You better go home now, Harold."

"Right."

He had made his way home then, robot-like, and

when he came into the front hall he had stopped and looked at himself in the mirror.

He had looked exactly the same. His face was a little redder maybe and a little shinier from being in the sun, but he was just the same. He had tried to imagine what Ada was feeling that would actually change the way she looked, but he could not. No one he loved had ever died or had even been real sick.

That was why it was so strange that he knew exactly how the Goat Man felt. He could have been the Goat Man. He suddenly wanted very much, before he left to make the phone call, to let Mr. Gryshevich know this. He wanted to say, "I know how you feel."

The trouble was that it seemed to Harold people were always saying that. They said, "I know how you feel," as easily as they said, "Thank you," or "Pass the butter," even if they did not know at all.

Harold recalled that when he was terribly hungry, unable to do anything but snarl, he was so hungry, then someone who was thin like his mom would say, "I know exactly how you feel, Harold, because I would like to have had an extra brownie for lunch." An extra brownie! Or, "I know how you feel about not getting on the baseball team, Harold, because one time when I was a girl I didn't get to be in Junior Chorus." Junior Chorus! How could anyone compare the baseball team to Junior Chorus? The baseball team was a whole different world.

Yes, he thought, people who know nothing are the first to cry, "I know exactly how you feel. I feel that way all the time."

Or maybe they did know, he thought with a sigh. Maybe other people had some extrasensory thing that was only at this moment being awakened in him.

All the same, he knew he would not say, "I know how you feel," to Mr. Gryshevich now. "I know how you feel, Mr. Gryshevich, because I too have been the extra hippopotamus." He could not say that. Ada and Figgy and the Goat Man would think he had had a concussion.

He said, "Well, I better get going."

He turned and began to walk away. Behind him the Goat Man spoke to Figgy, and Ada said something too. Harold glanced back. He wondered suddenly what was going to happen to the Goat Man now. There was no going back to the cabin, Harold knew that. By morning there would be no cabin. It would be flattened, scraped off the earth, burned. In a week the ground would be graded. In a month smooth white concrete would be where the cabin had stood. It would not even be possible to point out the exact spot.

"The cabin was *there*. No, wait a minute, wasn't it over here? No, *here*. No, wait, where *was* it?"

Maybe that would make it easier for the Goat Man. Harold didn't know.

He kept walking at the same pace until he caught

sight of the small grocery store in the distance. Then he began to walk a little faster. He began to plan the telephone call.

"Hello, operator," he would say, "this is Harold V. Coleman. I would like to make an emergency call."

In his mind his voice sounded deep and important. He remembered that when he was six years old people were mistaking him for his father on the telephone. Radio announcing seemed possible again.

"I would like first to speak to Dr. Arnold Harrison," he would say, "599-3324, and then directly to the emergency ambulance service."

He pushed open the old screen door of the grocery store. He did not look once at the little Dolly Madison cakes and the Twinkies on the bread counter. He did not look at the candy bars or the ice cream freezer. He did not even think about eating. He went directly to the telephone, deposited a dime, and dialed. His voice filled the store. "Hello, operator, this is Harold V. Coleman. I would like to make an emergency call."

MIDNIGHT

Harold and Ada sat on Ada's front steps, waiting for her father to come home and tell them how Figgy was. Harold's mother had called him twice, "Har-old! Bed-time!" But he still sat there with Ada. Harold thought that in a moment his mother would probably resort to tricks. "Har-old! Can-dy!" He thought of calling back, his voice deep with disdain, "I'm not hungry!" He glanced over at Ada and she was staring across the street.

Ada had always been something of a mystery to him. He wanted to ask what she was thinking because she had a remote, Egyptian look to her face. Just then, however, Harold's mother opened the front door again. "Har-old! It's twelve o'clock mid-night!"

"Mom, I'm not coming until I find out about Figgy," he called back. He folded his hands over his knees.

"Harold, you can find out in the morning."

"No."

"Harold, this is the last time I'm calling you."

"Good," he said quietly.

His mother shut the door, opened it again to let Omar out, and went back into the house. Harold glanced at his watch. He and Ada had been sitting here for two hours.

It had been just before ten o'clock when the ambulance and Ada's father had arrived at the scene of the accident. Harold and Ada had stood back while they put Figgy on the stretcher and into the ambulance. Then the Goat Man had climbed in too. And the ambulance had driven away.

"I'll take you two home before I go to the hospital," Ada's father had said. He had had to speak to them twice before they heard him. They had both been watching the ambulance disappear over the top of the hill. "Harold, you want to help me with these bikes?"

"Oh, yes, sir."

They had loaded the bikes in the back of the station wagon and Harold had crawled in the front seat beside Ada. Ada had talked to her father all the way home about the accident and about the Goat Man, but Harold had just sat there. For some reason there were two things he could not get out of his mind—the rabbit's foot lying in Figgy's hand and the way the Goat Man's eyes had looked the first time he saw them.

"It's always the little things that get me," he said now to Ada. He leaned down and pulled some grass out of his shoe.

"The little things?"

"Like Figgy's rabbit's foot. It's just a little thing, you know, but I remember exactly how it looked lying in his hand. I'm funny like that. All my life I'll remember Figgy because all my life I'll remember that rabbit's foot."

"Me too."

"I've always been that way. I get little things on my mind and I never forget them." He looked at her. "Remember me telling you about the other school I used to go to?"

"Northside?"

"Yeah, well, every December we would draw names for the Christmas gift exchange. This was a big thing. We would all run around like idiots saying, 'Who drew my name?' and 'What's he getting me, do you know?'"

"We did that at Dilworth too."

"Well, this year that I'm talking about, I found out that Bubba Joe Harris had drawn my name." He leaned forward. "It was a big disappointment because Bubba Joe Harris was the poorest boy in the school. I started getting desperate. I mean *I wasn't going to get a present,* I *knew* it, no present at *all.* I made endless trips to the pencil sharpener so I could look over the gifts under the tree. There was nothing for me. I would go back to my seat muttering, 'I *knew* he wouldn't get me anything.' I really got to hating Bubba Joe Harris."

Ada was watching him, leaning forward over her knees. She put her hair back behind her ears and said, "Go on."

"Well, the big day arrived. I had the only sullen face in the room. I was the only one not getting anything, see, and I hated Bubba Joe Harris as much as I ever hated anybody.

"This one girl, Helen McMannus, got to give out the gifts because she got all A's on her last report card, and she took about ten hours to call out the names and hand out the gifts and there was nothing for me. Nothing. All my Christmas treats—my Santa Claus cookie and my cup of hard candy—I couldn't even eat them because I was so sunk in misery.

"By this time I had seen that there weren't any more gifts under the tree and all around me people were bouncing balls and working puzzles and yo-yoing. I was the only inactive person in the room. It seemed to me then that the greatest blow a person could receive in his life was no gift at the Christmas exchange.

"I was looking down at my desk, probably fighting tears, when I heard Helen McMannus say, 'Oh, here's another gift. It's for Harold.' I jumped up like I'd been shot. For Harold! For me! I got something! I was ecstatic. In a moment I was going to be part of the yo-yoing, ball bouncing, puzzle-working world. I waited, wiggling with anticipation, and she came back and put down on my desk the tiniest present I have ever seen in my life. You never saw anything so tiny. I knew as soon as my eyes fell on it that Bubba Joe Harris had given me a gift-wrapped dime."

"A dime?"

He nodded. "Gift-wrapped in notebook paper, and let me tell you, Ada, there are not much sadder sights in the world than a gift-wrapped dime."

"Did you open it?"

"Yeah, I opened it and there it was, a Roosevelt dime. I can see it now."

"What did you do?"

"Well, I could see Bubba Joe looking at me, waiting for my reaction—one of the big things was watching people's faces light up when they opened your gift."

"I remember that."

"I had already missed seeing Carol Sweeney's face when she opened the Merry Make-up Kit I'd given her. But, anyway, I let my face light up and I said, 'Hey, you guys, look what I got—cash!' So I guess it went all right."

He looked at her. "But, you know, Ada, that gift-wrapped dime is going to be in my mind until I die, I know it will, one of the top ten saddest sights of my life." He shook his head. "Little things like that seem to go right inside me and stay."

"I'm that way too."

"It's like an arrow. It's like—" He broke off suddenly and sat erect. "Hey, here comes your dad."

Ada got up and ran across the yard to the driveway. "Come on, Harold." They got to the garage the same time as Ada's father and Ada opened the car door for him. "How's Figgy?" she asked.

"Oh, he's not too bad."

"How about his leg?"

"A break about two inches below the knee. No complications."

"And he's all right?" Harold asked.

"Yes. I would have liked to keep him in the hospital overnight, but he wanted to go home, and under the circumstances . . ." He trailed off.

"How about the Goat Man?" Harold asked.

Dr. Harrison shook his head. "Something's going to have to be done there."

"I know," Harold said.

"He reminds me a bit of my grandfather," Dr. Harrison said. "There are just some people that can't live in the city." He stretched his back. "My grandfather died of nothing but being brought to the city." He pushed open the door and went into the kitchen.

"What are you going to do, Dr. Harrison?"

"Well, I don't know. I'm going to try to find him

an old farm, maybe, a piece of land somewhere. He doesn't belong in that house across the highway."

"Dad, can Harold and I go with you to look at places?" Ada asked.

"I guess so."

"We could get him a couple of goats as a house-warming present," Harold said.

Harold had a picture of the five of them—Dr. Harrison, Ada, Figgy, the Goat Man, and himself—piling into the car together. To people who didn't know them they would look like a strange group, Harold thought, and yet they were linked together like a chain.

"Well, I better go home," Harold said.

"I'll call you in the morning, Harold, and we'll go over and see Figgy."

"We'll take the Monopoly."

"Right. See you tomorrow."

Harold crossed the dark street. Out of the shadows came Omar and he rubbed against the back of Harold's leg. "How you doing, Omar?" Harold scooped him up and put him on his shoulder. "Good cat." He set him down and Omar went into the bushes. Omar was too old to catch anything, but he still liked to wait in the shadows for moles and shrews and mice, his two claws digging into the dark, damp earth.

"Mom, I'm home," Harold called as he went into the house.

"Get to bed, Harold. It's late."

"Right."

Slowly he went up the stairs to his room. It was going to be a long time, he thought, before he understood this day. It was not like any other day in his life. It had been a day special enough to be celebrated each year. New Year's Day. Columbus Day. Goat Man Day.

Harold went into his room and got into bed. Suddenly he thought of himself as a grown man, a success. "Can you tell us, Mr. Coleman, anything in your life that had special meaning—any incident that influenced your life, any person?"

"Well," he would say, "there was the Goat Man."

"Who?"

"The Goat Man."

"*Who?*"

"Well, you see, one day this girl Ada and I were playing a game of Monopoly . . ." And while he was going over it in his mind, he fell asleep.

ABOUT THE AUTHOR

BETSY BYARS, one of the leading writers for young people, was awarded the Newbery Medal in 1971 for her novel, *The Summer of the Swans*. Mrs. Byars was born in Charlotte, North Carolina, studied for two years at Furman University in Greenville, South Carolina, and returned to Charlotte to earn a degree from Queens College. In 1950 she married Edward Byars, and while he was a graduate student at the University of Illinois, she began to write articles for *The Saturday Evening Post, Look,* and *TV Guide*. As her family grew, she started writing books for children.

Mrs. Byars and her husband and their four children live in West Virginia, where he is a professor of engineering at West Virginia University. She does her writing in the winter months; her husband's hobby is soaring, and her summers are filled with putting a sailplane together, taking it apart, taping and polishing it, and driving a thirty-five-foot trailer around the country.

Mrs. Byars's other books include *The Midnight Fox, The House of Wings,* and *The 18th Emergency*. Her most recent book was *The Winged Colt of Casa Mia*.